CLAUDIA, QUEEN OF THE SEVENTH GRADE

**Other books by
Ann M. Martin**

Leo the Magnificat
Rachel Parker, Kindergarten Show-off
Eleven Kids, One Summer
Ma and Pa Dracula
Yours Turly, Shirley
Ten Kids, No Pets
Slam Book
Just a Summer Romance
Missing Since Monday
With You and Without You
Me and Katie (the Pest)
Stage Fright
Inside Out
Bummer Summer

THE KIDS IN MS. COLMAN'S CLASS series
BABY-SITTERS LITTLE SISTER series
THE BABY-SITTERS CLUB mysteries
THE BABY-SITTERS CLUB series

CLAUDIA, QUEEN OF THE SEVENTH GRADE

Ann M. Martin

AN
APPLE
PAPERBACK

SCHOLASTIC INC.
New York Toronto London Auckland Sydney

*The author gratefully acknowledges
Peter Lerangis
for his help in
preparing this manuscript.*

Cover art by Hodges Soileau

ISBN 0-590-69212-7

12 11 10 9 8 7 6 5 4 3 2 1   7 8 9/9 0 1/0

Printed in the U.S.A.   40

First Scholastic printing, March 1997

CHAPTER 1

"Wait, Claudia," said Shira Epstein. "Wait. You mean you can't have a cross between a monkey and a horse because they're not in the same family?"

"I hope not," replied Josh Rocker.

Joanna Fried looked up. She was lying across her bed, leaning over the edge to read a homework assignment she'd put on the floor. "Imagine what their kids would look like," she murmured.

"My brother's a pig and I'm a human," Jeannie Kim remarked, braiding her hair. "And we're in the same family."

"Species," I corrected Shira. "Animals have to be in the same *species* to mate, not the same family."

"I thought they were the same thing," said Shira.

I shook my head. "No way. Species is a much more specific grouping. It goes like this: king-

1

dom, phylum, class, order, family, genus, species."

(Pretty smart, huh? Ahem. Thank you, thank you.)

"The further you go down the line," I continued, "the more things you have in common. Take us. We belong to the animal kingdom, but the class of mammals. We're in the same family as apes, I think. But species? Just us humans."

"Wait," Shira said, scribbling furiously, "what comes after phylum?"

As I recited the list again, Joanna, Josh, and Jeannie were giving me these wide-eyed, admiring looks.

"How do you know all this stuff?" asked Josh.

I shrugged modestly. "I just do."

The truth? I memorized the first letters of all those classifications — K, P, C, O, F, G, S — because they also stand for Kindly Pass Claudia Oreos, For Goodness Sake.

Pretty cool system, huh? Take something hard and make it simple, that's my motto. Relate your schoolwork to the things you really love. I, Claudia Kishi, happen to love Oreos. (I also happen to love every other kind of junk food known to our species, but Twinkies didn't fit in this memory trick.)

The only problem with the Kishi Learning System is that it makes me hungry. Luckily, junk food is not the only thing I love. In fact, it ranks second to art. Painting, sculpting, drawing, jewelry-making — I adore them all. In fact, I had tried to use artists' names to remember that long list — Kahlo, Picasso, Cézanne, O'Keeffe, Frankenthaler, Gauguin, and Seurat — but that was much harder.

Still, art helps me with all my other subjects. Social studies? I get to know historical characters by drawing them. Math? Well, I'm still working that out. Attractive borders around my homework sometimes keep me from falling asleep. (It's a start.)

As you can see, because of my superior learning system and high grades, I am invited to the houses of my fellow students to help them with homework.

(Yes, you may call with any questions related to the seventh-grade curriculum. I have my own private phone, listed in the Stoneybrook, Connecticut, phone book.)

Oh. One other small thing. I'm taking all my courses for the second time.

Why? Well, you see, I was born in the wrong year. I'm like my uncle Russ, who says he was meant to live a hundred years ago, because in his soul, he's a pioneer in the Wild West.

Me? I have the soul of a seventh-grader in the body of an eighth-grader.

Okay, okay, I was sent back a grade. There. Now you know.

I am thirteen years old. I started off in eighth grade, but I just couldn't hack it.

To be honest, hacking it has never been easy for me. It doesn't help that (a) my older sister, Janine, is a real genius, and (b) my parents have always expected me to be like her. It's not that I'm stupid, it's just that I see the world as an artist sees it, not as a scholar does. Geometry may not come easily to me, but I can make a beautiful cubist painting.

I felt devastated when I was told I had to repeat a grade. Destroyed. Humiliated. I wanted to curl up and die.

But so far, things seem to be turning out okay. My eighth-grade friends have not abandoned me, and now I have a whole batch of great new friends in the seventh grade. Shira, Joanna, Josh, and Jeannie. Plus, for the first time in my life, I feel caught up in my studies.

Not to mention the fact that my classmates actually think I'm smart.

"Okay, enough science." Shira slammed her notebook shut. Suddenly her jaw dropped. "Ahhh! Ahhh!"

"Shira, what's wrong?" Joanna asked.

"Ohhhhhh!" Shira moaned, slapping her forehead.

"Hunger pains," Josh guessed.

Jeannie, who had just opened a bottle of nail polish, quickly closed it. "Does this smell too much?"

"No!" Shira replied. "I just remembered. We're having a quiz on Stoneybrook government in social studies tomorrow."

Joanna rolled her eyes. "Shira, you know, you're like the boy who cried wolf."

"I'm not a boy!" Shira snapped.

"She means you should chill," Josh translated.

"Josh," Shira said with a deep sigh, "no one says 'chill' anymore."

"They should," Josh remarked. "To you."

Shira stuck her tongue out at him. "Joanna, you told me you don't allow boys in your room."

"Josh doesn't count," Joanna said.

"Thanks a lot!" Josh cried out.

Crazy. That's what I like about my new friends. I've only met them this year, but I feel as if I've known them my whole life. Shira is the number-one stress case of Stoneybrook Middle School. She can work herself up to a frenzy about the slightest thing. Luckily, she doesn't take herself too seriously. Look at her cross-eyed and she giggles. She's tall and skinny, with coppery red hair and blue eyes.

Joanna is the seventh-grade president. She's a real presidential type, too — very smart and take-charge, focused but easygoing. She has long brown hair, dark eyes, and an open, friendly face.

Josh is . . . well, Josh. Just mention his name, and people roll their eyes or groan. That's mainly because he's always trying to be funny. (Actually, he *is*. Cool, maybe not. But funny, definitely.) Anyway, he's short and kind of cute, with wavy black hair and a goony smile.

Jeannie is a very special friend. We have a lot in common. Like me, she's Asian-American, although her family is Korean and mine is Japanese. Like me, she does well in school (well, a lot better than me, actually, and it's her first time through seventh grade). Like me, she is crazy about clothes, but in a different way. She tends to follow the styles in *YM* and other magazines. I believe in Found Fashion.

What's Found Fashion? I find funky-looking castaway things in thrift stores, and I fashion them into cool outfits.

That day, for instance, I was wearing an old leopard-pattern blouse, sixties-style hip-huggers, a wide headband, and plain black flats with white ankle socks. It was a lot like an outfit I had seen in the mall for a zillion dollars, but I put it together for practically nothing.

I was pulling up my ankle socks, listening to Josh and Shira argue, when I caught a glimpse of Joanna's clock: 5:08.

I had twenty-two minutes. Five-thirty was starting time for my Monday Baby-sitters Club meeting. (What's the Baby-sitters Club? I'll tell you about it later.) Joanna's house is a ten-minute walk from club headquarters (my bedroom), so I had only twelve minutes left — five, if I expected to do a little cleanup beforehand.

I told you my math was improving.

"Well, guys," I said, closing my science book, "I am out of here."

"So soon?" Shira groaned.

Josh was whispering something in Joanna's ear.

"We said we wouldn't tell her now," Joanna whispered back.

"Why does it have to be a secret?" Josh asked.

Huh?

"Tell me what?" I asked.

"Have a wonderful meeting," Josh said solemnly.

I put my hands on my hips. "That's not fair! I caught you, now you have to tell me."

Joanna and Josh exchanged a glance. "But

7

you might be disappointed if it doesn't happen," Joanna said.

"If *what* doesn't happen?" I asked.

"If you don't win," Josh answered.

This was making me nervous. Had they entered me in a contest? Signed me up for a quiz show?

I looked at my watch. "I have three minutes. Explain, please."

"Josh and I have nominated you for Queen of the Seventh Grade," Joanna explained.

"Yyyyess!" Shira shouted. "Great choice!"

"If I-I-I-I were Queeeeeen of the Seventh Graaaaaaade!" sang Josh, in his best Cowardly Lion imitation.

I burst out laughing. What a ridiculous idea.

Josh beamed. He thought I was laughing at his joke.

I should explain. Stoneybrook Middle School has this incredibly old-fashioned custom. I think it dates back to World War I, possibly the Middle Ages. Whatever. Anyway, each grade — sixth, seventh, and eighth — elects a King and Queen. Basically it's a popularity contest. The winners go onstage and look embarrassed during a "coronation" assembly. Then they have to select "attendants" (usually their best friends). They're all supposed to help plan the prom together. (We call it a prom because it's one of the biggest dances of the year. But it's *not* as big a deal as a high school prom.)

On prom night, the King and Queen march in to a rock tune, wearing these dumb robes and crowns. They have to dance to the "class song," while everyone screams, "Kiss! Kiss!" It sounds kind of dorky, I know. At my last seventh-grade prom, the King tried to kiss the Queen, but she ran off, calling for cootie protection.

Real mature, huh?

"You have got to be kidding," I said.

"No way," Joanna replied. "You're perfect, Claudia."

"Perfect?" It was now 5:12. "First of all, I hardly know anybody in seventh grade —"

"We'll fix that," Josh said. "Tomorrow we start a major ad campaign for you. All the media will be at school. We've got *People* at 8:00, MTV at 8:15, CNN — "

"Second of all," I barged on, "you three would be much better candidates than me."

"Too much work," said Shira.

"Too much attention," said Jeannie.

"The class president is disqualified," said Joanna.

"Wrong gender," said Josh.

"Anyway, Claudia," Joanna went on, "we already nominated you. You don't hate us, do you?"

Hate was too strong a word. I guess I should

have been annoyed. I mean, it would have been nice if they'd consulted me, even though I probably would have declined.

But you know what? I was kind of tickled. Not about the Queenship, or whatever you call it. About being nominated. About the fact that my friends cared enough to enter my name.

Right after I returned to seventh grade, I started feeling a little lonely. It's hard to meet kids when you're sent back. The seventh-graders were either a little afraid of me, or they thought I must be stupid. (Well, not all of them, but I thought they did.) Who knew? As Queen nominee, I would probably meet a lot more seventh-graders. And I sure didn't stand a chance of winning, so I didn't have to worry about the corny ceremonies and stuff.

The way I figured it, I had nothing to lose.

"I don't hate you," I said with a smile. "I'm kind of glad you did it. Thanks."

"Yeaaaa, Queenie!" Shira said.

"Not so fast," Josh piped up. "Your one requirement is you have to insist on me as King!"

"Can it, Rocker," Jeannie said.

"If I make it, Josh," I said, stuffing my homework into my backpack, "which I won't, then you can have the first dance. Whether you're King or not."

"If I-I-I-I were Kiiiing — "

As I slipped out of the room, the girls were pelting Josh with pillows.

I couldn't help smiling. Seventh grade was turning out to be fun. I was doing pretty well with my schoolwork, I had good buddies, I was even running for Queen.

And now I was on my way to see my absolute best friends in the world.

Not a bad life, huh?

CHAPTER 2

*C*lick.

As I entered my room, Kristy Thomas was hanging up my phone. "You're alive," she said.

"I think so," I replied.

"I just called nine-one-one," Kristy explained. "I was worried."

I dropped my pack on my bed. "Kristy, what is wrong with you? I'm not even late! I don't want cops and medics and people running all over the house — "

Kristy burst out laughing. "Joke! That was a baby-sitting call."

I yanked open my dresser drawer. I pulled a bag of marshmallows from behind a pile of underwear and threw it at Kristy.

"Hooooo-ha-ha-ha!" Kristy blocked her face with her arms. The bag bounced off and fell, spilling marshmallows onto the floor.

Abby Stevenson rushed in from the direction

of the bathroom. "Did I miss a fight? If I did, you have to start again."

I squatted on the floor, scooping up marsh-mallows.

"You know, this is a waste of perfectly good sugar."

"*You* threw them," Kristy reminded me.

"She has another bag behind the shoe boxes," Abby said.

"How did you know?" I asked.

Abby shrugged. "A good guess."

Honestly, you'd think they would show some respect to the official permanent host of the Baby-sitters Club.

All right, I promised I would tell you about the club, so here goes.

First of all, Kristy doesn't always pull dumb pranks. She just likes to make me feel guilty for being late, even for almost being late. As president and founder of the Baby-sitters Club, she calls the meetings to order, and she hates lateness.

We meet three times a week, Mondays, Wednesdays, and Fridays, from five-thirty until six. During that half hour, our phone rings off the hook. (Isn't that a weird expression? I mean, if the phone is off the hook, it *can't* ring.) Our clients are Stoneybrook parents who want the highest-quality, most reliable baby-sitting around (well, it's true). How do they know about us? Sometimes we advertise. And, of course, happy parents tend to spread the word to other parents.

Our clients love the convenience we offer. At first, though, some of them aren't sure how their kids will adjust to having several different sitters, as opposed to one or two regular ones. But we handle that easily. Kristy makes us write about each job experience in our official BSC notebook. That way we keep each other up-to-date about all our charges (the kids we baby-sit for). So far, it's worked great. Parents don't complain about multiple sitters.

Kristy invented the Baby-sitters Club one afternoon when neither she nor her two big brothers, Charlie and Sam, were available to baby-sit for their little brother, David Michael. Kristy's mom called all over town for a sitter, with no luck.

Big Problem, thought Kristy. It needed a Big Solution. And she came up with one: a central agency with one phone number for a group of sitters.

Guess which friend of Kristy's had a private phone available? *Moi*. At first, the club was just Kristy, me, and two other members: Stacey McGill and Mary Anne Spier. But, like most of Kristy's Big Solutions, it grew Bigger and Bigger. We became a huge success. Now we have

14

ten members — seven regular, two associate, and one honorary.

I am the vice-president of the club. My duties include (1) taking the baby-sitting calls that come in during off-hours (grrr), (2) being a charming host, and (3) providing lots of junk food.

I take (3) extra seriously. My room is a hiding place for the worst foods known to humankind — cookies, chips, pretzels, and chocolates galore. (I have to keep it all hidden. My parents would go ballistic if they actually saw the stuff.)

Kristy, as president, is the real brains of the group. Her motto is simple: "Find the clients, keep them happy." She dreams up great publicity schemes. If there's a festival or fair in Stoneybrook, Kristy organizes a BSC booth, complete with free baby-sitting advice and BSC fliers. Plus, she never stops thinking of ways to keep kids happy. If the BSC treasury has a little extra money at the end of the month, she puts together events for our charges (especially around holidays). She even formed a team called Kristy's Krushers for little kids who loved baseball but weren't part of Little League.

Kristy is a huge sports fan. She follows all the teams. She once told me she could spend an entire day shagging fly balls and not tire out. I had no idea what shagging meant. I pictured her ripping the stuffing out of the ball and combing it into a seventies hairstyle.

What's Kristy like? Short, loud, and bossy. Also reliable, strong, and consistent. Casual too. She wears sweats, T-shirts, and sneaks all the time. Fashion, for Kristy, is . . . well, not a high priority.

I've tried suggesting that Kristy put a little variety into her wardrobe. It's like asking a tree to grow hair. I guess I can understand why she likes the predictability. Her life has been a roller coaster. Years ago, when Kristy lived across the street from me, her dad up and left the family. Kristy didn't show much emotion (except anger), but I know she was deeply hurt. Life became pretty rough, and Kristy worked hard to help her mom. Recently, Mrs. Thomas met and married a really nice guy named Watson Brewer, who happens to be a millionaire. For Kristy, it was like winning the lottery. *Zoom*, she and her family moved to Watson's mansion across town.

The Brewer/Thomases nearly fill up the place now. Start with Kristy's mom, Watson, Kristy, and her three brothers. Then add Watson's kids from his previous marriage, Karen and Andrew, who live there during alternate months. Kristy's grandmother, Nannie, lives there year-round. She helps take care of Emily

Michelle Brewer, Kristy's little two-and-a-half-year-old adopted sister who was born in Vietnam. Throw in a puppy, a cat, and a few other pets, and you can picture what life is like there.

Sort of like my room at 5:28 on a Monday. Crazy and crowded.

As I picked up the last of the fallen marshmallows, the other BSC members began arriving with a flurry of hellos. Mary Anne Spier and Stacey McGill sat cross-legged on my bed. Mallory Pike and Jessi Ramsey plopped themselves down on the floor next to Abby.

Kristy was now sitting in my canvas director's chair, juggling marshmallows.

"Hey, I'm doing it!" she shouted.

As my clock clicked to 5:30, Kristy caught one of the flying marshmallows in her mouth. "Doof mifftiff — " She quickly chewed and swallowed. "*This meeting* will come to order!"

Kristy never — *never* — misses that 5:30 call.

Reaching into her backpack, Stacey pulled out an old manila envelope. "Dues day!"

That reminded me of something. I reached behind my headboard for a hidden bag of candy. "Pay Days!"

The grumbling was canceled out by the cheers.

Yes, we do have to pay dues out of our earnings. Some of the money helps pay for my phone bill. Kristy's oldest brother, Charlie, gets

17

a gas allowance for driving Kristy and Abby to meetings. And we always need a little cash for special events and for Kid-Kit items (Kid-Kits are boxes of toys, books, games, and kid-friendly stuff, which we often take with us on our jobs).

As you might have guessed, Stacey's our treasurer. She is an absolute math whiz, who recently led the SMS Mathletes team to a state championship. Personally, I think growing up in New York City helped her. Have you ever asked a New Yorker how to find someplace? Everything is measured in numbers: "Go three stops on the Number One, switch to the uptown Three and take it to Ninety-sixth, walk two crossstown blocks and three downtown blocks to One Hundred Ten West Ninety-third . . ."

Numbers weren't all Stacey picked up from the city. Her fashion sense is totally NYC, totally cutting-edge. She can practically smell what the year's next hot outfits will be. I adore the way she dresses — sleek and urban, lots of black, which really sets off her blonde hair and fair skin.

How did she end up in a nice suburban place like Stoneybrook? Divorce. After her parents split, they gave her a choice: stay in NYC with her dad or move to Stoneybrook with her mom. Well, Stacey had already lived here for awhile, when her dad's company had transferred him to Connecticut temporarily. She had joined the BSC and made such fabulous friends, she just had to return. (Boy, was I glad she did. Stacey and I are best friends.)

In one major way, Stacey and I are opposites: she cannot eat sweets. Stacey has a condition called diabetes, which means her body goes seriously bonkers if she eats refined sugar. She could pass out or become terribly ill. Don't worry, though. As long as she eats regular meals and gives herself daily injections of this stuff called insulin, she can lead a perfectly normal life.

Okay, now that you know the club's finances and eating habits, I'll tell you about the O.P. (Kristy-talk for "Operating Procedure"). When a parent calls during meeting hours, we take the information about the job and turn to our secretary, Mary Anne. She's in charge of the record book. It contains a calendar, full of all our baby-sitting appointments and personal schedules — family events, doctor and orthodontist appointments, after-school activities, and so on. For any given day, Mary Anne can figure out exactly who's available. We discuss who should take the job, then call the client back. But knowing who's free is only part of her job. She also keeps an updated client list in the back of the book, including addresses and phone numbers, rates charged, and any important information about the children.

Organized? That's Mary Anne's middle name. But that's probably not the first thing you'd notice about her. She's sweet and shy, and she's the best listener and most generous friend. She also tends to cry a lot. Her copy of the book *Mrs. Fish, Ape, and Me, the Dump Queen* is warped from tears.

Maybe that's because the narrator of the book lost her mom. Mary Anne's mom died when Mary Anne was a baby. Her dad raised Mary Anne by himself, with super-strict rules. He insisted she wear these conservative, little-girl outfits right through seventh grade.

Boy, has Mary Anne's life changed since then. For one thing, she has a cool, short hairstyle now and dresses in neat, preppyish clothes. For another, her family has more than doubled in size. What happened? Well, Richard loosened up. And he became so attractive that his old high school sweetheart married him.

Okay, it wasn't quite that simple. You see, his former girlfriend, Sharon Porter Schafer, had been living in California for years. She and Richard had completely lost touch. When the Schafers divorced, Sharon moved back to Stoneybrook with her daughter and son, Dawn and Jeff. Dawn ended up joining the BSC, and when she and Mary Anne figured out their parents' little secret, you can guess what happened. Fireworks. Romance. Wedding bells. Mary Anne gained a sister, brother, and mom. Plus a new address, when she and her dad moved into the Schafers' rambling old farmhouse.

Happily ever after? Not really. Dawn became homesick for California and her dad, and moved back (following in the footsteps of Jeff, who had already done the same thing). Mary Anne was pretty upset, but she and Dawn talk all the time, and Dawn visits a lot. (She's the honorary member I mentioned earlier.)

Besides, Mary Anne's social life keeps her busy. She has a boyfriend named Logan Bruno, who's cute and athletic and funny. He's also a great baby-sitter — great enough to join the BSC! As an associate BSC member, he doesn't usually come to meetings, but he takes jobs whenever he can (which isn't too often, because he's involved in after-school sports).

Our other sports-minded member is Abby. She's not a jock or anything, just an incredible natural athlete. Kristy is a little jealous of her, but Abby takes it with a sense of humor. In fact, she takes everything with a sense of humor. Since she joined the BSC, our meetings have become laff riots.

Abby used to live on Long Island. She, her mom, and her twin sister, Anna, moved to

Stoneybrook right around the time Dawn left. What timing. We needed sitters badly, and we asked both sisters to join. Abby agreed, but Anna said she wouldn't have enough time. She actually practices the violin two hours a night. (Can you imagine?)

Two things you'll notice about Abby: her hair, which is thick and curly and seems to have a life of its own; and her allergies, which make her sound as if she has a cold all the time. She reacts to dust, shellfish, dogs, strawberries, and a million other things (fortunately, *not* junk food). Abby also has asthma, so she has to carry inhalers with her at all times.

Abby does have a quieter side. You see it whenever her dad is mentioned. He died in a car wreck when she was nine, and the memory is still sharp and painful. She was especially sad he couldn't attend the twins' Bat Mitzvah. That's a coming-of-age ceremony for thirteen-year-old Jewish girls. Everyone in the BSC attended. Boy, was I impressed. Not only was it beautiful and moving, but Abby and Anna had to recite in Hebrew! (I don't know what they said, but it sounded great.)

Abby, by the way, is our alternate officer. She fills in whenever one of the main officers is absent.

Our junior members are Jessi and Mallory. They are eleven years old and in sixth grade.

Their parents refuse to let them baby-sit at night, but we manage to fill up their afternoons and weekends with jobs.

Jessi and Mal are best friends. You can usually find them gabbing about horses. Ask either one about the tiniest detail of any *Saddle Club* book, and they'll give it to you instantly, in unison. If you want to stay on their good sides, *don't* ask them whether they like being the oldest in their families. They're both convinced that parents are much more lenient with younger siblings. (Jessi has a younger brother and sister, and Mal has seven younger siblings.)

Two peas in a pod? Not exactly. Jessi's African-American, elegant and graceful, an incredibly talented ballerina. Mallory's white, short, and not very athletic, and determined to become a professional writer. (Can you see it now? *Baby-sitters Club,* the musical — book and lyrics by Mallory Pike, choreography by Jessica Ramsey, and award-winning sets designed and painted by Claudia Kishi!)

The minor characters in our play would be Logan Bruno and Shannon Kilbourne. Well, minor in stage time but not importance. I've told you about Logan already. Shannon, our other associate, attends a private school called Stoneybrook Day School, where she's involved in tons of after-school activities.

23

Now you know all my best and oldest friends. Who I never see in school anymore, now that I've been sent back to seventh grade. (Sigh.) Even our lunch periods are at different times. I look forward to BSC meetings soooo much now.

I don't even mind Kristy's bossiness.

"Okay, new business?" Kristy asked, then immediately answered, "Yes. Mrs. Addison called before the meeting started. You know how the Addisons have their own business now, and work at home? Well, for the next month, they have this big outside meeting on Thursdays. Starting this week, they'll need a sitter after school for Sean and Corrie. Can we give her a schedule? Do we want to take the job?"

Let me explain that last question. Awhile back, Sean set some small fires in the public library, mainly because he was upset about having to be part of a Readathon. The BSC caught him in the act and turned him in. He apologized tearfully, but we hadn't heard from the Addisons since.

"They've been in family therapy," Stacey said. "Maybe things are better now."

"Does anyone have a problem with this?" Kristy asked.

We all shook our heads, and Mary Anne be-

24

gan writing a schedule. "Me this week, Abby next . . ."

Kristy called back and confirmed the next month with Mrs. Addison. When she hung up, I said, "Okay. I have some new business. Big, serious news. You won't believe it."

"You have a math test coming up," Kristy guessed.

"I'll tutor you," Stacey volunteered.

"Nope," I replied. "I'm totally caught up."

"I know!" Abby exclaimed. "You met Picasso."

"He's dead," I informed her.

"Then that *is* big news!" Abby said.

Hopeless.

"I have been nominated," I barged on, "for — are you ready for this? — Queen of the Seventh Grade. Ta-da!"

"Yeaaaaa!" Mallory cheered.

"Cool," Jessi said.

"You must be joking," Kristy remarked.

"I'm not," I replied. "Joanna and Josh put my name up — "

"Who and who?" Abby asked.

"They're my friends," I explained. "I mean, I know it's ridiculous, but I think it's hilarious."

"Imagine," Stacey said. "Well, even if you were elected, you couldn't accept it."

"Why not?" I asked.

"That would be cheating," Stacey answered. "You're thirteen, Claudia. Technically, you're an eighth-grader."

"I am? Well, I wasn't allowed to go to the eighth-grade Halloween party. I'm not allowed to eat with the eighth-graders. Officially, I'm as seventh-gradish as you can be."

"What kind of time commitment is this . . . Queenship?" Kristy asked.

"Kristyyyy," I said. "This is a *goof*. A *joke*."

"You mean, you weren't really nominated?" Mary Anne asked.

"I was, but I'm not going to win or anything," I answered. "I just think it's funny. Why are you all taking this so seriously?"

Kristy smiled. "For your sake, Claudia. We'd hate for you to actually have to kiss a seventh-grade boy or anything."

"Depends on the boy," Jessi remarked.

"Eeeeew, *Jessi!*" Mallory said.

They both dissolved into giggles.

Rrrrring!

Mary Anne picked up the phone, and we were back to baby-sitting. I didn't bring up the Queen of the Seventh Grade again. No one seemed to think it was as goofy as I did.

Oh, well. It didn't really matter.

I still thought it was nice to be asked.

CHAPTER 3

"So, let's move now from *Call of the Wild* to *Hatchet*," said Ms. Chiavetta. "How do we compare them? Anyone?"

Point of view, I thought.

From the seat behind me, Joanna said, "I liked *Hatchet* much better."

"Haaaa-*chet!*" a boy sneezed from the back of the room.

"Bless you," said Ms. Chiavetta. "*Why* do you suppose you liked it?"

"*Haaaa-CHET!*" Now the whole group of boys in the back of the room was giggling like crazy.

Joanna looked befuddled. I tried to send her a telepathic message that said, *Point of view.*

"How about point of view?" Ms. Chiavetta asked.

(Brilliant of me, huh? Not really. I'd been through this discussion the year before.)

"Uh . . ." Joanna said.

"Through which character do we experience the story in each book?" Ms. Chiavetta asked. "Claudia?"

"In *Hatchet*, it's the boy, Brian," I replied. "In *Call of the Wild*, it's the dog, Buck."

"*Buck-buck-buck-buck* . . ." clucked one of the boys quietly.

"*HAAAAAAAACHET!*"

I turned around. The sneezer, a boy named Mark Jaffe, sat in the last seat of my row. All around him, kids were cracking up. Mark had this deadpan look, as if he were hanging on Ms. Chiavetta's every word.

The biggest gigglers were a couple of the girls, Loretta Jorgensen and Jennifer Kline. They were looking at Mark as if he were a rock star who happened to have floated into the classroom.

Puh-leeze.

I mean, yes, Mark is cute. He has high cheekbones and long brown hair that flops across his face. His eyes are a deep, luscious brown and he seems older, more like a high-school kid. But looks aren't everything, and all his muttering in the back of the class can be pretty obnoxious.

"We get the joke, Sneezy Snyder," Ms. Chiavetta said patiently. "No need to repeat it."

"Sorry," Mark said. "Allergies."

"Anyway, how does the point of view

change the way we feel about a story?" Ms. Chiavetta droned on. "Ron?"

The most positive thing about being sent back: things are definitely easier the second time around. Last year I felt forced to read those two books. It was about as much fun as a math assignment. Reading them again this year, I could not believe they were the same books. I couldn't put them down.

"Well, it's like the story is . . . you know, viewed with a different . . . point, like," Ron Tibbets answered. "What was the exact question again?"

Ugh. I was eager to move past the easy stuff and really talk about the plot. I checked the clock on the wall. It was already eleven seconds until the end of class.

Eleven seconds until lunch.

My stomach began churning. *This* was the call of the wild. Forget about English.

"We will pick up this discussion tomorrow," Ms. Chiavetta said. "For those of you who haven't finished — "

Rrrringggg!

Everyone stood at once, gathering up books.

I heard something smack to the floor. Out of the corner of my eye, I saw a paperback face-down near Mark's right foot. All at once, Loretta and Jennifer stooped to pick it up. Loretta reached it first. Red-faced, she returned

29

it to Mark, while Jennifer giggled like crazy.

"So mature," Joanna murmured as we left class.

"Why is he so popular?" I asked.

"He is pretty cool, you have to admit," Joanna said with a shrug. "I heard that Loretta nominated him for King of the Seventh Grade."

"He doesn't need to be King," I said. "He already has people waiting on him hand and foot."

"Well, I guarantee he's a shoo-in."

"Hi, Claudia!" a voice piped up from across the hallway. "Good luck!"

A red-haired girl waved to me. I smiled and waved back. "Who was that?" I whispered.

"Bonnie Lasher," Joanna replied. "I told her in math that you were running for Queen. She said she'd vote for you."

"Really?" I felt all shivery. I didn't even know Bonnie.

As we turned left toward the cafeteria, the smell of over-boiled broccoli wafted toward us. (*Whoosh*. There went the old appetite, out the window.)

Near the cafeteria doors, Shira was trying desperately to close her locker. Joanna and I ran to help her.

"What do you have in there?" Joanna asked,

throwing her weight against the narrow metal door.

"Nothing!" Shira replied. "Just, you know, clothes and books and food and stuff."

"Maybe if you move some junk around . . ." Joanna opened the locker, and two cans of chicken noodle soup crashed to the bottom.

"Snack?" I asked.

"My mom put them in my backpack," Shira said with a sigh of frustration. "She says I should set them up on a table or something in the middle of the front lobby and start a food drive."

"Why?" I asked.

"You know my mom," Shira said, rolling her eyes.

I didn't, really. Although I had seen her once on the local news, leading a protest against something. And you couldn't miss the seventeen bumper stickers on her car, all from environmental and humanitarian groups.

"Ready?" Joanna said, leaning her shoulders toward the open door. "One . . . two . . . three!"

With a lunge, the three of us managed to slam the door shut.

"Just promise you'll help me open it later," Shira murmured.

Together we entered the Chamber of Mush. Josh was standing at the end of the lunch line with a group of friends. When he saw us, he pretended to hold up a fake microphone. "And here we are in the lunch line with the Claudia Kishi fan club. Don't look now, folks, but here she is, the leading candidate for Queen of the Seventh Grade!"

"Will someone turn him off?" Shira said.

"Hey, we were just talking about you," Josh said, turning to his friends. "You guys are voting for Claudia, right?"

Three guys I barely knew nodded.

"I bribed them with baseball cards," Josh said in a stage whisper.

We all took trays and slid them onto the track. I was between Shira and Joanna.

"Anyway," Shira said, "my horrible obnoxious cousins from Westchester go to this school that's having a food drive for charity. Well, my mom thinks this is fantastic and wants me to start one here. The thing is, the drive is sponsored by some supermarket that isn't even in Stoneybrook! I mean, it's a good cause, sure — but how am *I* supposed to organize this thing?"

As we slid along, picking up food, a voice behind me yelled, "Yeah, Claudia the Queen!"

Over my shoulder I saw a boy named Neil punching the air.

"Boy, are you ever Miss Popularity," Joanna said.

"I mean, I would *like* to do it," Shira continued as we walked to a table, "but I don't have the time, with homework and the school newspaper and yearbook and all. What do you guys think?"

"*That's* Claudia," Josh was saying loudly to a table full of kids I hardly recognized. "Trust me, she's perfect."

I didn't know whether to blush or bop him on the head.

Jeannie was already sitting at a table by the window, deep in conversation with two other girls. We sat down across from them. Shira kept trying to talk about her dilemma, but she wasn't having an easy time. For one thing, the conversation was going in a million different directions. For another, about four kids came up to tell me they were going to vote for me.

By the time the end-of-lunch bell rang, Shira still hadn't decided what to do. Joanna and Jeannie were busy discussing whether the chicken sauce contained Elmer's Glue, and Josh was reminding kids left and right to vote for me.

"Uh, Josh," I said as we all headed for the door, "you don't have to do this, really."

"You're new, Claudia," Josh said. "You need visibility. You need P.R. Leave the dirty work to me."

"I don't know what has gotten into him," said Jeannie with a laugh.

Josh blushed. "I love proms."

As usual, Joanna and Shira went one way toward their classes. Jeannie, Josh, and I headed the other way.

We ran into Kristy, Stacey, Abby, and Mary Anne walking around the corner.

I have to admit, seeing my BSC friends on their way to eighth-grade lunch is painful. As we greeted each other, I could feel a tug in my chest. I missed going to lunch with them. I missed our conversations. Every day I wondered what they were talking about, what jokes I was missing, what gossip I'd be the last to hear.

"Mary Anne is having second thoughts about the Addisons," Stacey said. "She thinks Mrs. Addison is hiring us to teach Sean a lesson."

"A form of torture, in other words," Abby added.

"I say, go for it," Kristy declared. "They called us. We agreed. A job is a job."

I looked toward Jeannie and Josh. They were staring off in the other direction.

"This kid, Sean?" I said to them. "He caused some major trouble because he set fire to some library books. Now his mom wants us to sit regularly for him."

"Uh-huh." Jeannie smiled politely.

Josh looked at his watch. "Are you coming to class?"

"What's for lunch?" Kristy asked me.

"The chicken is disgusting," I replied. "But Jeannie liked the sandwich — "

I looked over at Jeannie. She was reading the Heimlich maneuver poster across the hall.

"Last call, Claudia," Josh called out.

"Thanks, Claudia," Kristy said as she and my other BSC friends walked inside the cafeteria.

" 'Bye," I said.

Weird. I felt like a secret agent or something. My eighth-grade friends and seventh-grade friends didn't seem to want to talk to each other.

Rrrringggg!

Oh, well. Time to run to class. Another assignment in the Double Life of Agent Claudia Kishi.

CHAPTER 4

The day before the election, I was a wreck.

I know, it sounds stupid. I mean, it wasn't as if I were in some contest on worldwide TV. At thirteen years old, I shouldn't be worried whether a bunch of seventh-graders wanted me to be their prom queen.

But I was.

For more than a week, my friends had continued their "campaign" for me. Joanna and Shira had been pretty casual about it. But Jeannie was all gung-ho, and Josh was . . . Josh. Honestly, I think he will run a U.S. presidential campaign someday. He must have introduced me to a hundred classmates.

I kind of enjoyed that. I was meeting kids I might not have met otherwise. Most of them said they'd vote for me.

But hey, let's face it, I didn't have any high hopes. I was running against two incredibly popular girls: Abigail Leib, who's modeled for J. Crew, and Duryan Weinstein, the class vice-president. If one of them didn't win, the other would. And that would be just fine with me.

So why couldn't I sleep the night before the vote? Every time I closed my eyes, I heard that dumb song you always hear at graduation ceremonies. (Kristy calls it "Pumpin' Circumstance," but I doubt that's the real title.)

When my alarm woke me up, I was dreaming about Queen Elizabeth of England. She and I had switched clothes. I was wearing this dark, subdued, foulard dress that hung on me like a popped balloon. Her hair was tied to one side with a scrunchie and she was dressed in Spandex pants, a Hawaiian shirt with ED'S DINER stenciled across the breast pocket, and a pair of Doc Martens.

"How do I look?" the Queen was asking me as I awoke.

I jumped out of bed and stumbled to the mirror. My hair looked like a snake pit and my face was all wrinkled from my pillow.

"Auggggh!" I screamed.

Some Queen I was. The Queen of the Dead.

I switched into serious Bad Face Day mode. I showered, yanked, and combed, and generally forced myself to look human. It must have worked, because when I ran outside to the corner where I meet my friends every morning, neither Mary Anne nor Stacey fainted with fright.

On our walk, we didn't talk about the vote. We met Jessi and Mal along the way. They wished me good luck. But that was it. Very low-key. I figured they knew I was nervous. I was grateful for that, but it would have been nice if they'd been a little more excited. Oh, well.

We went our separate ways inside school. I met Jeannie outside homeroom. She was leaning against the wall, her face set in a scowl.

"They're cheating," she muttered.

"Good morning to you too," I joked.

"Sorry, it's just that I overheard Abigail say she's been promising to buy kids ice cream if they agree to vote for her. She is so *phony*."

"Jeannie, it's okay," I said as reassuringly as I could. "Whatever happens, happens."

"How can you stay so calm?"

Good acting, I wanted to say. My stomach was on spin cycle.

We walked into class together. In the back of the room, Mark Jaffe was hunched over his desk, his head cradled in his arms.

"Beauty sleep?" I asked.

Loretta spun around angrily. "Shhhh," she said.

"He's tired," Jennifer explained.

"Poor baby," Jeannie said under her breath.

The class soon filled up, and Mark managed to rouse himself. Some of his buddies were slapping him on the back, shouting, "Long live the King!" and "Mark is number one!"

He wasn't the only one being fussed over (harrumph). Joanna, Josh, and Shira each stopped by to wish me good luck. Jessi and Mallory did too. That was a nice surprise. (I was a little embarrassed when Josh announced, "Anyone who doesn't vote for Claudia will be expelled," but I got over it.)

"All right, settle down, we have a lot to do!" announced our homeroom teacher, Ms. Pilley, the moment after the bell rang.

As she slammed the door, I had a slight sinking feeling.

I didn't know what it was at first. Then I realized — none of my eighth-grade BSC friends had stopped by to wish me good luck, the way Josh and the others had. It was weird. I mean, it's not as if the eighth-grade homerooms are miles away.

Ms. Pilley was handing out ballots. "These will be anonymous," she said. "Do not show your vote to anyone else . . ."

I took a deep breath. No use feeling hurt. I had to be realistic. *I* was the one who insisted the Queenship was no big deal. *I* told everyone I had no chance to win. What was I expecting? Wild enthusiasm?

How could they know what I was feeling inside? I wasn't even sure myself.

The three Queen nominations were printed next to the three Kings. I checked off my name, of course. Then I looked at the choices for King: Mark Jaffe, Frank O'Malley, and Tom Blanton.

I didn't know Frank or Tom. But Tom's name reminded me of Thomas Hart Benton, an American painter I adore. So I voted for him.

"Ready?" Ms. Pilley asked.

Grunt, grumble, shuffle, nod, everyone replied.

She collected the ballots and put them in a pile on her desk. "My best to both of you, Claudia and Mark," she said with a chuckle. "I guess if you win, we'll have to roll a red carpet down the aisle."

"Or put a love seat in the back, so they can *kiss!*" called a boy named Len Judson.

The whole back of the classroom thought that was hilarious. Of course, someone just had to make loud kissing noises.

I turned around and glared at the kissers. I caught a glimpse of Mark. He was just sitting there, stretched back with his feet on his desk, smiling. I'm not completely sure, but I think he gave me a wink.

Can you believe it? As if kissing him was the number-one most fabulous dream I could ever have. What a conceited creep.

"Quiet!" Ms. Pilley said. "As you probably know, the ballots will be counted today and the winners will be announced at an assembly during last period."

"Yyyyesss, no math!" shouted Loretta.

Mark let out a big yawn. "Can we go home if we don't want to be there?"

Titter, titter, giggle, giggle.

The bell rang a moment later. As I was packing up, Mark walked by and bumped into me.

"Excuse you," I said.

"Sorry," Mark murmured, giving me a long look. "Are you Claudia?"

I nodded politely. He may have been cute, but he sure didn't seem too bright. I mean, he'd been hearing my name practically every day.

I thought he was going to wish me good luck or something. Instead, he smirked, gave kind of a snort, and left.

For a moment I imagined what it would be like to be Queen to Mark's King. The thought was so nauseating, I put it out of my mind.

I remained in school, but my mind was somewhere just north of the Twilight Zone. Especially late in the day.

My last-period class is gym. Our teacher, Ms. Rosenauer, told us to stay in street clothes and led us to the assembly. (I'm a terrible athlete, but for once I would rather have been playing basketball. At least I could run around and not feel so tense.)

The auditorium sounded like the monkey cage at the zoo. Everyone seemed so excited. Joanna's and Shira's last-period class walked in with mine, so we managed to sit together. From a farther spot, Josh tried to start a cheer of "Clau-dee-*A!* Clau-dee-*A!*" but his teacher shut him up.

Shira and Joanna talked to me a mile a minute. I have no idea if my responses were in any recognizable language — but boy, was I glad my friends were with me.

Onstage, next to a microphone on a stand, stood two tacky-looking thrones. Actually, they were green padded-vinyl metal chairs from the school office, covered with velvet bunting, fake sheepskin rugs, and dangling doodads probably left over from someone's Christmas tree. On each seat was a gold plastic crown studded with colored-glass stones.

"DAAAAAAAA-DADADAA-DAAAAAAAAA-DAAAAA..."

From the loudspeakers blared "Pumpin' Circumstance," and I had visions of Queen Elizabeth again.

Mrs. Hochberger, an English teacher, stepped up to the mike. "Hear ye! Hear ye!" she called out. "Villagers, courtiers, and scholars, lend me your ears!"

"Oh, please," said Joanna, breaking into laughter.

"As seventh-grade advisor to ye royal prom committee," Mrs. Hochberger continued, "I hereby convene the Sixty-first Annual Stoneybrook Middle School Seventh-Grade Prom Coronation!"

Wild yelling.

If my stomach could have fallen any further, it would have been trapped in the seat cushion.

"As you all know, the crowning of King and Queen has been a cherished SMS institution since the Great Depression," Mrs. Hochberger went on.

"Zzzzz," snored Shira.

"The lucky young winners will be very respected people around the school," Mrs. Hochberger said. "They will need to choose attendants — ladies- and men-in-waiting — who will do their bidding in preparation for the big event. This year, because of the gym's after-school-use schedule, the seventh-graders will have their prom early, at the end of this month. So our royalty will be very busy . . ."

"Wake me when they count the votes," Mark's voice murmured from somewhere behind me.

Mrs. Hochberger made each of the candidates stand up. I dreaded my turn. When I had to stand, I felt like such a goon. I heard Mark mutter something to one of his friends, and when I glanced at them they were grinning at me. Puh-leeze.

After we sat down, Mrs. Hochberger went on and on about the wonderful catering our prom was going to have, and the fabulousness of the custodial staff. Finally she announced, "And now, without further ado, I exercise my privilege of announcing the names of the newly elected King and Queen of the Seventh Grade!"

Gloop. My stomach rose right out of the seat and lodged itself in my throat.

Shira and Joanna both put their arms around me and squeezed.

Mrs. Hochberger pulled an envelope out of her blazer pocket. "For King . . ." She ripped the envelope open and pulled out a sheet. "Uh . . . hmmm."

She lifted her glasses. She made a big show of not being able to read it.

The whole audience was hooting, urging her on.

Mrs. Hochberger turned the sheet upside down and grinned. (What a ham.)

"The crown goes to Mark Jaffe!" she exclaimed. "Come on up, King Mark!"

I could not help groaning. I don't think Mark heard me, though, because most of the audience was shrieking with excitement. Loretta and Jennifer looked as if they were about to weep with joy.

Mark made a big show of waking up, blinking his eyes, and looking mildly amused. Yawning, he stood up and sidled toward the aisle while kids pounded him on the back.

He shuffled slowly up to the stage, giving casual nods to a few friends, as if he were heading to lunch.

Mrs. Hochberger hugged him when he climbed onto the stage. He made a face. Then she put the crown on him. From his expression, you would think she'd just covered his head with lice.

He plopped himself down on the "throne" to wild applause. Smirking, he clenched his fists in a triumphant Rocky-style pose.

I nearly barfed.

Okay, he was cute. I had to admit that. The more I saw him, the better he looked. But really. The kids were treating him like a movie star. How childish.

And he seemed so, so self-satisfied.

"Who will join King Mark on the throne? Let's find out!" Mrs. Hochberger began opening another envelope.

"Eeeeeeee!" Shira was squealing.

At least I think it was her. It may have been my stomach.

"And the winner is . . ."

45

CHAPTER 5

I was feeling faint. Nauseous. I gripped my armrests.

Mrs. Hochberger was fumbling with the paper. The comedy routine again.

Not funny! I wanted to scream.

"Ihsik Aidualc!" she announced.

Foooosh! I hadn't realized I'd been holding my breath until it all rushed out.

I was off the hook. Disappointed, yes. But relieved, too. Must have been a write-in candidate. Someone I'd never met.

I heard a stereo "Huh?" from Shira and Joanna.

Mrs. Hochberger turned her sheet around and gave that grin again. "Oops. Had it backward. The crown goes to . . . Claudia Kishi!"

Clank.

My jaw hit the floor.

Shira and Joanna shrieked so loudly I felt as if I'd stepped inside a police siren. The corny music was blasting away. I saw Josh's baseball cap fly into the air. Below it, Josh was dancing and five-slapping like crazy.

I felt hands pushing me. "Go, girl, go!" Joanna was saying.

I stumbled over knees and feet. I could see arms reaching upward toward me in high-five position. I don't know if I returned them or not. I was in a fog.

"Haaaaail, Claudiaaaa Kiiiiiiishi," bellowed Josh to the tune.

I tripped up the steps to the stage and nearly broke my wrists stopping my fall. (How graceful.)

"Congratulations," Mrs. Hochberger said as she placed the crown on my head. It was so big, it slipped over my eyes.

Lovely. Now everybody was laughing.

I kept my sense of humor. I lifted the crown and placed it at a slight angle on my head (hey, a little style never hurts).

As I sat on the "throne" next to Mark, he was cracking up.

"What is so funny?" I asked.

"You have floor dust on your elbows and knees," Mark said.

Trying not to look *too* dorky, I placed my arms demurely by my sides and crossed my legs.

Mark grabbed some of the velvet bunting

and began wiping the dust off my crossed knee. That made everyone laugh again.

At that moment, I could not have hated him more. "Stop!" I hissed.

He gave me a goofy smile. "Didn't want you to be embarrassed."

"Stand, please, Your Highnesses!" Mrs. Hochberger commanded.

Mark and I rose to our feet, and Mrs. Hochberger clasped heavy velvet capes around our necks. The capes were old and smelled of moth balls.

All the seventh-graders were standing now. Standing and *applauding*, for goodness sake. Some of them were eyeing the exit. I could tell they thought this was the nerdiest moment of the year. But a lot of kids were truly excited (probably the ones who voted for us).

Mark gave a royal wave and said out of the side of his mouth, "I feel like a total fool."

Aha! An honest, human emotion!

"Me, too," I confessed.

I joined the wave. We were waving in unison, left, right, left, to the beat of the music.

Soon the whole audience was swaying like a mirror image.

That was way cool.

Mrs. Hochberger was having a hard time keeping a straight face. "Uh, before we're all dismissed back to class, I want to remind you that the Queen and King will be choosing their attendants from among all of you. Thank you!"

As the classes started filing out, Mrs. Hochberger pulled up a chair next to Mark and me. "The whole idea of this," she said softly, "is to stir up excitement about the prom. Don't go overboard bossing kids around. Just have fun with it."

"What exactly do we do with the kids we pick?" I asked.

Mrs. Hochberger shrugged. "You know, they help out with the prom plans . . ."

"Like, making food and decorating and picking music?" I pressed.

"Well, no," Mrs. Hochberger replied. "The administration has a budget for that. But on prom night you arrive early and pose for yearbook photos. Usually a photographer from the *Stoneybrook News* is there . . ."

"You mean," said Mark, "we don't do nothing!"

"You don't do *anything*," Mrs. Hochberger corrected him, then winced. "That's not what I meant. You don't do *nothing*, Mark — "

"That's what I said," Mark shot back.

"What I mean is . . ." Mrs. Hochberger's smile was stiffening. "Well . . . it's more like . . . an honor, I guess," she stammered. "A tradition."

Kind of a dumb tradition, if you asked me. A waste. If you have two leaders and a bunch of attendants, why not put them to work? (I know, I know, you think I've been hanging around Kristy too long.)

I was about to say something to Mrs. Hochberger, but she looked at her watch and said, "Go ahead to your classes. I'd like to have a meeting with you both after school on Monday."

Mark groaned. "After school?"

Mrs. Hochberger managed a half smile. "Be a sport, Mark. Now run along, before everyone's gone."

We took off our crowns and capes and walked out together.

"What a joke," Mark muttered.

I shrugged. "If you think so, then apticate," I said.

"You mean, *abdicate?*" he asked with a grin.

A mocking, superior grin. If there's one thing worse than a cute, obnoxious boy, it's a cute, obnoxious boy who thinks he's smart.

"Whatever," I snapped.

"I mean, if we're the King and Queen, we should do stuff. Like make the food. My dad works in a restaurant. He could help us out."

Well, well.

An Idea. A real, honest-to-goodness Idea from the mind of Mark Jaffe. And one that I agreed with. Would wonders never cease?

"You mean, a food committee," I said. "I was thinking of that. We should have other committees too. My friends and I are really good at organizing stuff. They're mostly eighth-graders, though. Thirteen, like me."

Mark nodded. "I didn't know you were that old."

"It's not *old* — "

"Were you left back or something?"

I glared at him. "I don't think that's any of your business — "

"Sorry. I mean, I just asked because *I* was."

"You were what?"

"Left back. In third grade. I have a learning disability. I was a late reader."

"Really?" I asked.

We were at the auditorium doors, and Josh was barreling through. "Yyyyyo, Queenie!" he yelled.

He put his arm around my shoulders and escorted me into the lobby. "No flash photos, please! Autographs after school!"

I could hear Mark cracking up. But I couldn't see him. We were both surrounded.

Jeannie, Shira, Joanna, and I fell into a group hug. Josh tried to organize a throne of linked arms to lift me, but it didn't work. My back was being slapped so much, I felt like a tom-tom. *Everyone* was congratulating me.

You know what? Through all of it, I could not stop grinning. Corny tradition or not, being Queen was great. I loved it.

As I walked with my class back to gym, I spotted Mark with his class. He smiled at me and waved.

I smiled back. I felt a little guilty. I mean, I had been kind of snobby to him. Jerky, obnoxious people can be human too.

Sometimes.

During the rest of gym class, I could not stop thinking about ways to organize the seventh-grade prom. Forget about being a useless Queen. I was determined to create the All-New, Queen Claudia's Authentic Student-Run Prom. I would organize committees. Drag Mark's dad into the food preparation. Create fabulous decorations, maybe even costumes. Send fliers home to ask for volunteers.

I felt as if I'd just been to see the Wizard of Oz. He'd given me a crown — and I'd discovered the Kristyness hidden inside me.

I couldn't wait to run my idea past Kristy herself. After class was over, I sped to the front door and waited for my BSC friends.

Stacey was the first to arrive.

"Guess what?" I squealed.

"You're Queen," Stacey said with a smile.

"How did you know?"

Stacey shrugged. "It was either that, or you were just promoted. Why else would you look so ecstatic?"

"I know. You think it's dumb. I did too, at first. But now I — " Out of the corner of my eye I could see Kristy and Abby approaching. "Stacey, hold my train."

"Your *what?*"

"The train of my dress. Pretend!"

I walked toward Kristy regally, like Queen Elizabeth inspecting the Royal Middle School, waving slowly to my subjects on each side, chin held high.

"Look, Kristy," Abby said. "Stacey has created a Claudia robot."

I gave her a Look. "That's my Queen walk!"

Kristy looked shocked. "You won?"

"Yup!"

"What did you do, bribe them with Yodels?" Abby asked.

"Ha ha," I said.

"But — but you're an eighth-grader!" Kristy exclaimed.

I put my fists on my hips. "Thank you both for being so happy for me."

"I was kidding," Abby said.

Jessi and Mal were running toward me now. "We heard you won!" Jessi shouted.

"Yeeaaaa, Claudia!" Mal called out.

It was nice to see some respect. And when Mary Anne arrived, she actually had tears of joy in her eyes.

But Mary Anne had to run off to the Addisons'. And Kristy and Abby had to catch the bus before I could say anything about my great plan.

I mentioned the plan to Stacey, Jessi, and Mallory. They thought it sounded fine, but we didn't talk about it much.

On the way home, Jessi told us all about a ballet performance she was preparing for. In great detail.

My Queenship wasn't mentioned again.

Oh, well, I guess royalty just ain't what it used to be.

CHAPTER 6

Thursday

Before sitting for the Addisons, I took all the books out of my Kid-Kit. No, I wasn't afraid Sean would burn them. I just thought they'd bring back awful memories of the Readathon.

My memories were sure strong. When I rang the Addison's bell, I was shaking . . .

Mary Anne was still cautious about being with Sean. I don't blame her. How many kids do you know who would actually burn books in public places just because they didn't want to be in a Readathon? I mean, he said he was sorry, and his parents seemed dedicated to working with him, but still . . .

As Mary Anne waited on the Addisons' front stoop, Sean peered out the living room window.

Sean is ten years old, with wavy light brown hair and dark eyes. He's pretty quiet, and he doesn't show much expression.

Well, that's not totally true. Mary Anne was discovering that he could put on a world-class sneer.

She saw him mouth the words "Oh, no!" and sink out of sight.

Nice welcome, huh?

The front door swung open. Mr. and Mrs. Addison did not seem happy. Behind them, Sean was stomping away angrily.

"Come in, Mary Anne," Mrs. Addison said. "May we talk for a minute?"

They're going to fire me, Mary Anne thought. *They hired me so they could fire me.*

Swallowing hard, Mary Anne walked into the living room and sank into the sofa cushions. Mr. and Mrs. Addison sat in easy chairs opposite her.

Thump-thump-thump, went Sean's footsteps up the stairs. His voice carried down from his room, muffled: "I *hate* brabbarabba."

Sean's nine-year-old sister, Corrie, popped into the living room. With a wide smile, she said, "Hi, Mary Anne! You know what Sean told me? He eats baby-sitters for lunch!"

"Corrie, please do your homework," Mr. Addison said.

"He is so mean," Corrie said, skipping away.

Mr. Addison smiled tightly. "Sean is feeling a little resistant to baby-sitters in general, Mary Anne. Don't take it personally."

"He has a lot of anger," Mrs. Addison explained. "He used to keep it all bottled up. He would express it in antisocial acts — you know, like the Readathon incident."

"Since we've been going to family therapy," Mr. Addison went on, "he's been learning to express his anger verbally."

Mary Anne smiled and nodded. But inside she was having a cow. Express his anger verbally? That was the last thing Mary Anne needed. She absolutely hates confrontation.

When the Addisons left, Mary Anne took several deep breaths and slowly walked upstairs to the kids' bedrooms. Corrie's door was open. She was lying on her bed, reading Beverly Cleary's *Henry and Beezus*.

"Hi, Corrie," Mary Anne said. "Just wanted to let you know that if you need me — "

"Ssshhh, I'm at the best part," Corrie said.

Mary Anne slunk away. Down the hall, Sean's bedroom door was closed. Mary Anne could hear his fingers clacking away at a keyboard. She raised her arm to knock on his door.

"Oowww! Unnh! Unhh-unhh-uh-uhhhhh!" Sean growled.

Mary Anne froze.

"Will you stop that?" Corrie shouted.

"What?" Sean called back.

"I said, will you stop groaning? I'm reading!" Corrie replied.

"I wasn't groaning!"

"What were you doing, Sean? Singing along with your headphones?"

Silence.

"MARY ANNE! SEAN'S NOT SUPPOSED TO LISTEN TO HIS RADIO WHILE HE DOES HOMEWORK!"

Sean's door crashed open. Mary Anne jumped away. Sean ran past her as if she weren't there.

He burst into Corrie's room, steaming. "You ugly little frog breath pig face!"

"GET OUT OF HERE!" Corrie cried.

By the time Mary Anne reached the room,

Sean had grabbed the book out of her hand. "Oh, I think this baby book is sooooo funny!" he said, pretending to read it. "Tee hee hee."

"Sean, please," Mary Anne said. "Give her back the book."

Sean flung the book on the floor and stalked back to his room.

Corrie's lips were curled under in pre-cry mode. "He bent my book!"

"So sit on it!" Sean shot back, disappearing behind his door.

Corrie was in tears. Mary Anne sat on the bed next to her and gave her a hug.

"I was j-just — " said Corrie between sniffles, " — telling you what Mom and Dad said. That's all."

"I know," Mary Anne said softly. "Your feelings are hurt. You deserve an apology."

"Ha!" came Sean's voice.

"Go yell at him," Corrie said.

Mary Anne stood up. Her heart was racing. *He is only a ten-year-old boy,* she kept repeating to herself. *Be patient.*

She walked bravely to Sean's room. His door was not quite latched, so she knocked and pushed it open a crack. "Sean?"

Sean was sitting at his desk with his headphones on. He quickly took them off and turned around on his swivel chair. "What's the password?"

"Sean, I'm not trying to intrude on your privacy," Mary Anne said. "But I'm your sitter, and I have to follow house rules — "

"I won't use the headphones anymore, okay?" Sean said. "I just wanted to hear one song. Now, since you didn't tell me the password, get out of here so I *can* do my homework."

Mary Anne stood her ground. "Sean, you're not being very nice."

"Yeah!" called Corrie.

"Then will you *please* get out of here?" Sean asked. "And will you *please* tell my sister to brush her teeth because I can smell her breath from here?"

"Hey!" Corrie protested.

SLAM! Sean closed the door in Mary Anne's face.

Bursting with rage, Mary Anne kicked the door down and screamed at him.

Just kidding. But she did open the door again and said, "Sean, you are out of line. I will let you do your homework. But I insist on two apologies. You have been rude to me and mean to your sister."

Sean rolled his eyes. "Sorry," he grumbled. Then he slouched into Corrie's room, repeated "Sorry," and slouched back.

Oh, well. It was better than nothing.

Mary Anne ducked into Corrie's room again.

"Call me if he gives you any more trouble," she whispered.

Back downstairs Mary Anne went. She quickly set up her own homework on the kitchen table.

She was halfway through her math assignment when Sean gave a loud, strangled-sounding cry.

Zoom. Mary Anne bolted upstairs and rapped on Sean's door. "Are you all right?"

"I hate this!" Sean wailed.

Mary Anne opened the door. Sean was sitting at his desk, slumped over an open textbook.

"Hate what?" Mary Anne asked.

"Math!" Sean shot back. "I can't do it."

Mary Anne couldn't help but laugh. "I thought it was something serious."

"Password?" Sean snapped.

"Look, I can help you with your math, Sean," Mary Anne volunteered.

"Not unless you know the password," Sean protested.

"It wouldn't matter even if you did," Corrie said from her room. "He changes it!"

"Phew! Yeccch! The breath! Gag me!" Sean yelled.

"Make him apologize, Mary Anne!" Corrie demanded.

"She's right, Sean," Mary Anne said.

"Why are you bossing me around, anyway?" Sean snapped. "You're not my baby-sitter. You're Corrie's."

"He thinks he's such a grown-up!" Corrie yelled. "But he's really a baby! Sean is a baby! Sean is a baby!"

"I hate you!" Sean leaped out of his chair.

Mary Anne stood firmly in the doorway. She had had enough.

"Sit down!" she commanded.

I think Sean was shocked. He skidded to a stop.

Mary Anne gulped. She was a little surprised at herself too.

"Corrie, that time you provoked your brother," Mary Anne said over her shoulder. "Kindness has to go both ways."

"See, she needs a baby-sitter, not me," Sean said, sinking into his bed. "Why do I have to have one?"

"Is this what's bothering you?" Mary Anne asked. "What's wrong with having a sitter?"

"My parents are only going to be gone a little while, right?" Sean asked.

"An hour and a half."

"So what can happen in an hour and a half? I can be here alone with Corrie. I'm ten!"

Mary Anne sat on the floor. "Lots of ten-year-old kids have sitters, Sean. The Pike triplets are ten, and we sit for them."

"No, you don't. They're, like, assistants. They told me."

(Boy, was that ever a stretch of the truth.)

"Sean, have the triplets been teasing you about having a sitter or something?"

"Well, not them . . ." Sean's eyes were beginning to well up now. "This other guy says if I have a baby-sitter, I must be a baby."

"That's just silly — "

"To you it is. But I'm the one everyone makes fun of."

Mary Anne gave Sean a reassuring smile. "Look, I'll promise to keep this between me and your family, okay? No one in Stoneybrook Elementary has to know you have a sitter."

"Right. They're probably spying on me." Sean stood up and walked back to his desk. "Can I do my homework now?"

"Okay," Mary Anne said. "Call me if you need help."

Sean grunted. Mary Anne quietly turned and went back downstairs to the kitchen.

Before long the Addisons returned. "Well, well," Mr. Addison said. "Everything sounds nice and peaceful."

"Not!" bellowed Sean, clomping down the stairs. "Mary Anne was talking to me while I was trying to do my homework."

"He's lying!" Corrie yelled, running after him. "Sean was being mean!"

"I'd be much nicer if I didn't have to have a baby-sitter," Sean said. "I don't need one."

"Sean — " Mary Anne began to protest.

"It's true!" Sean said. "Mary Anne didn't do a thing to help me. From now on, I should baby-sit all by myself!"

"We'll consider that, Sean," Mr. Addison said.

Corrie looked horrified. "No way!"

"Now, would you both mind if we talked to Mary Anne alone?" Mr. Addison asked.

The two kids left the kitchen, bickering.

Mary Anne was speechless. She fought back tears.

Mrs. Addison smiled at her sympathetically. "Don't you worry. We know you did a fine job."

"It's — it's a tough age, I guess," Mary Anne said. "And he's being teased at school."

"We know," Mr. Addison said with a sigh. "Maybe we can figure out a way to make him feel more responsible."

"We'll talk to him, Mary Anne," Mrs. Addison said. "By next week, he'll feel better. You'll see."

"Thanks," Mary Anne said.

Inside, however, she was saying something else.

She was saying, thank goodness I *won't* be the one to see.

CHAPTER 7

"Tell them you need a royal scepter," Josh said. He slammed his locker shut and began walking down the hall with Shira, Jeannie, Joanna, and me.

"Josh, that's ridiculous," I replied. "I can use the rest rooms like everyone else."

Josh looked at me blankly.

Joanna stifled a laugh. "*Scepter*, not septic. You know, one of those big staffs with a ball at the top and tassels hanging on it?"

Duh.

"Oh, right, *that* scepter," I said, trying not to sound like a total nincompoop. "What are those things for, anyway?"

"Hitting peasants over the head, I think," Shira replied.

"That could be useful at the prom," Jeannie suggested.

"Don't pick your nose over the punch bowl

— *whack!*" Josh said. "Stop hogging all the cheeseburgers — *whack!*"

We turned the corner. Kids swarmed around us on their way to the front lobby, gabbing and shouting.

School had just ended. It was Monday, and I was on my way to Mrs. Hochberger's classroom, for my first official prom meeting.

My mind was spinning. All weekend I'd been thinking about my little plan, and it had grown. Queen Claudia's prom was going to be the greatest event in SMS history. Not only would it be organized and run by students, but it would be a charity fund-raiser.

I know, now you really think I'm morphing into Kristy. Wrong. I admit I'd brought some of my ideas up at Friday's BSC meeting. Kristy had said it sounded "fine," but she hadn't wanted to talk about it much, because it wasn't "club business." So, you see, it was all my brilliant idea.

I tried to bring it up with my seventh-grade friends, too. But they had some ideas of their own. I was hearing every one of them.

"A royal steed," Jeannie suggested. "That's what you need."

"Hey, you're a poet, and you don't know it!" Shira piped up.

"But your feet show it," Josh said. "They're Longfellows. Get it?"

Jeannie lunged after him. *"Bring me my scepter!"*

As they ran down the hall, giggling, Joanna said, "Have you ever been to a Renaissance festival? People dress up in clothes from the Middle Ages and talk in old-fashioned English accents — 'Canst thou guidest me to thy nearest privy?' and stuff like that — and you can do crafts and shoot crossbows and watch jousts. We should have something like that in school."

"Crossbows? Uh, let's not and say we did," I suggested.

"Well, maybe not that, or the jousting," Joanna conceded. "But we can do the rest."

Shira was cracking up. "Right, Joanna. And wear togas while we work on ye old mainframe computers."

"They didn't wear togas then," Joanna protested.

"I have a better idea," Shira said. "Call my parents, Claudia. *You* arrange for our school to join the food drive, and then I won't have to hear about my obnoxious cousins again."

"I already thought of that," I replied.

"You did?" Shira exclaimed. "Oh, bless you, my leech."

"I think it's *liege*," Joanna said.

We were now approaching Mrs. Hochberger's room. Jeannie and Josh were returning to us, out of breath and laughing.

"Fare thee well," I said, holding out my arm. "Thou may kiss the royal knuckles."

Shira grimaced. Joanna and Jeannie rolled their eyes. Josh, however, planted a big wet one.

"Ewwww, Josh!" I cried.

"You asked for it," he said.

Wiping my hand on my pants, I ducked into Mrs. Hochberger's room as my friends shouted good-byes.

Mrs. Hochberger was busily marking papers. She looked up in surprise. "Oh! Our meeting! Oh, dear, I'd forgotten!"

"I can come back another time," I volunteered.

"No, sit down, my fault." Mrs. Hochberger pulled up her papers and looked toward the hallway. "Where's Mark?"

"I don't know, but while we're waiting, I wanted to tell you about an idea I had."

I cleared my throat and collected my thoughts. I had to make this sound fabulous.

"Okay," I began. "I was thinking to myself, 'Claudia, what's the point of having a Queen and King? Just some old-fashioned custom? Can it be something more? Something that would make the prom more interesting and fun?' "

"Well, Claudia, to be honest, the titles are sort of honorifics," Mrs. Hochberger said.

"Yes, and I feel very honorific to have been chosen. But I figured out a great answer. Step one? Get rid of attendants — "

"Whoa, hold it right there," Mrs. Hochberger interrupted. "You need people to help you."

"Right. But picking attendants is unfair. I mean, Mark and I will just pick people we know. It'll be like a clique. What about the other kids who would really love to work on the prom? It would be much more fair to have sign-up sheets. I bet lots of people will want to be involved."

Mrs. Hochberger smiled patiently. "I just don't know if there's that much to do. The school takes care of most of the preparation. You just need to make a few decorations."

"So we'll form a decoration committee. But it'll be just one of a whole bunch of committees. I mean, why should the school do everything? Take the catering. That must be so expensive. We can have a food committee that decides on a menu and prepares the food. Mark's dad works in the restaurant business, and he can help. Now, we have to make sure everyone attends, right? So we have a publicity committee that designs fliers and makes regular announcements over the PA. Then we have a music committee that puts together a great tape and picks a DJ. An award committee thinks of funny prizes — you know, weirdest haircut, most likely to be confused with an Elvis sighting, stuff like that. It'll be so much fun!"

Mrs. Hochberger was chuckling. "Claudia, you're being very . . . ambitious."

Clunk, went my heart. "You hate the idea."

"No, I didn't say that. Actually, I think it's wonderful. But I have to warn you, you're taking on a lot. Other Queens have come to me with similar ideas in the past, and they've never quite worked out."

"Those Queens weren't me!" I replied. "Besides, Mark and I are in total agreement."

"Well, in that case," Mrs. Hochberger said, "I suppose we can try it."

"Ohhhhh, thanks, Mrs. Hochberger!" I wanted to throw my arms around her and jump up and down. But I didn't. I kept my Queenly dignity.

At that moment, King Mark the Tardy shuffled through the doorway, with his hands in his pockets. "Yo, am I late?"

"I was talking about the plan we made," I said excitedly. "Sit down. There's a part I haven't told you about."

"Wait. What's the part you *did* tell me about?" Mark asked, slumping into a chair.

Ugh.

I went through the whole thing again. He looked as if he'd never heard a word of it.

When I reached the part about the sign-up sheet, he said, "Whoa. Whoa. I'm the King, right? So I should have an equal say. And I say, forget about the sign-up sheets and stuff — "

"But you agreed, remember?" I persisted. "On the way out of the auditorium? *You* were the one who suggested the food committee."

"Yeah, but it was more like, 'Wouldn't it be great if,' not 'Let's do it,' " Mark said. "You know, hypocritical."

"Hypothetical," Mrs. Hochberger gently corrected him. (Personally, I thought Mark had it right.)

"Whatever," Mark snapped. "Besides, what am I going to tell my attendants? 'You're fired'?"

"You already picked attendants?" I asked.

Mark shrugged. "Duke, wizard, earl, wenches — "

"Wenches?" I said.

"That was what we were supposed to do, right?" Mark asked.

"Pick wenches? You are so sexist, Mark Jaffe!"

"No, pick attendants! Besides, it's a joke, Claudia. That's what this whole thing is. It's for fun, not some serious Girl Scout project!"

"There you go again!" I said.

"Okay, Boy Scout too. You know what I mean." Mark sighed. "I thought I was doing the right thing, Claudia. If you had this big plan, why didn't you call me?"

"Okay, okay, maybe I should have," I admitted. "I should have assumed you'd have amnesia."

"Please," Mrs. Hochberger said. "The King and Queen must not fight."

Mark grinned. "Yeah, or we'll be in the tablets."

"-*loids*," I said.

"Who's Lloyd?"

"*Tabloids!* Can I mention the other part of my plan?"

I was practically shouting now. Honestly, I wanted to throw him out the window.

"Go ahead," Mrs. Hochberger said.

"Well, my friend Shira was telling me about this food and clothing drive in her cousins' school. I thought we could have one too. As part of the prom. A special committee could set up a drop-off corner in the gym."

Mark let out a big groan.

"What's wrong with that idea?" I shot back. "Did you promise all your old clothes to one of your attendants?"

"Very funny," Mark said. "Claudia, your idea's cool, but it's so much work."

"No, it isn't!" I insisted. "The committees do the work. We just do the planning."

"Like what?" Mark asked.

"Figuring out what the committee should do, giving them deadlines — "

"But . . . but I can't — "

"Checking up on them from time to time, troubleshooting — you know, *planning*."

"I have trouble planning my lunch!"

That I did not doubt.

Stalling. That's what he was doing. Trying as hard as he could to ruin my plan.

Well, I wasn't going to let him.

"I want to try this, Mark," I said firmly. "But I can't do it if you don't help. Say no, and we'll have the same old-fashioned stupid prom they've always had. We can walk around with crowns and look dorky and pose for pictures and be really embarrassed. Say yes, and we'll create a prom we can be proud of. Involve everybody. Raise money for charity."

"But my attendants — " Mark protested.

"They can be the first to sign up for committees. You can still call them dukes and wizards if you want." I leaned back in my chair and exhaled. "It's all up to you."

"Ahem," Mrs. Hochberger said. "Has everyone forgotten about me, the lowly faculty advisor?"

Yikes. "You agree, right?" I asked.

Mrs. Hochberger nodded. "But I feel it's

only fair for you to let Mark think about it."

Mark let out a sigh like Hurricane Bob. "Okay, okay, let's go for it."

"You mean it?" I asked.

Mark shrugged. "It's what you want."

"What about you?" I asked. "Will you help me?"

"Hey, a King is a King. I can't let down my subjects." He picked up his backpack and headed for the door, grumbling, "As long as you do most of the work."

I had a feeling I was in for an uphill battle.

CHAPTER 8

"Is that — could that be — oh, wow, may I have your autograph, Your Majesty?"

Josh's voice took me by surprise as I left school. "What are you doing here?" I asked.

Josh shrugged. "I was looking at the school wall. I thought I saw some fossils in the stone. Can I walk you home?"

"You are so weird."

"Just because I want to walk you home? Claudia, we must have a talk about your self-esteem."

I was in no mood to joke. I was so angry at Mark Jaffe, I could barely see straight.

I headed away from the school, hands in my pockets.

"Thanks, Josh, I'd love to have your company," Josh said, falling into step beside me.

"He is such a jerk," I muttered.

"Total jerk," Josh agreed.

"Conceited and stupid," I continued.

"If he had twice as many brains, he'd be a half-wit."

"A big blowhard."

"Ugly, too."

I glowered at the pavement. Our footsteps echoed dully in the cold March air.

"Claudia?" Josh asked.

"What?"

"Who are we talking about?"

"Mark Jaffe!"

"Oh, why didn't you say so? I wouldn't have been so nice!"

That did it. I couldn't help laughing.

"Aha! A smile!" Josh said. "Don't try to hide it!"

"Okay, okay. You win. You stopped me from feeling totally miserable. Are you happy?"

"I'll take what I can get. So, what happened with Queen Claudia's Royal Service Plan?"

"Well, let me put it this way. You were right about the scepter. I should have one, to bash Jaffe over the head."

"I'd buy tickets to see that. So would a lot of people. You could make a fortune."

I described everything in detail — the meeting, my idea, Mark's reaction. Josh hung onto every word. By the time I finished, he was angry, too.

"I'm on your side," Josh assured me. "And

so are Shira and Jeannie and Joanna. If Mark is a total zero, we'll make up for him."

As we crossed Burnt Hill Road, I glanced at Josh. Under his green woolen watch cap, his ears stuck out at an odd angle. He looked like an earnest little chipmunk.

I smiled. "You know, you're a great friend, Josh," I said. "I'm really glad I know you."

"Really?" Josh's voice was practically a squeak.

"I mean, I used to feel so awful about being in seventh grade. But not anymore. Because if I hadn't been sent back, I wouldn't have met you guys."

Honnnk! Honnnnk!

With a wheeze and a pop, Charlie Thomas's car barreled around the corner. (Actually, *car* is a kind word for it. It's more like scrap metal on wheels.) Abby and Kristy were waving to us out the open windows.

"Want a lift?" Kristy asked.

"Nahh, it's so close," I replied.

"Let us out here, Jeeves," Abby said to Charlie.

The car pulled up to the curb. As Abby and Kristy climbed out, Stacey's voice called to us from up the block. "Hiiii!"

"Hi!" we all called back.

"You're welcome!" Charlie yelled sarcastically as he drove off.

"Uh, well, I guess I'll be going home," Josh said.

Abby gave him a puzzled look. "Is this — ? Did we meet — ?"

"This is Josh," I said. "He's one of my friends."

At that point, Stacey was running toward us, her hair blowing in the wintry breeze. I could see Josh's mouth practically drop open in awe. "Hi," he said. "Well, uh, I guess I better be heading back now."

"Thanks for walking with me, Josh," I said.

"Any time," Josh replied, heading back toward the school.

"Where does he live?" Abby asked me.

"Centennial Avenue," I answered.

"That's at the other end of town," Kristy observed.

Abby raised her eyebrows. "Hmmmm, walking you home, huh?"

"Cute little guy," Stacey remarked.

"Watch it, Stace," Kristy warned. "Did you see the way he looked at you?"

"Ssshhh, you'll break Claudia's heart," Abby said.

That made everyone crack up.

Except me. For some reason, it didn't seem funny. Not at all.

The jokes about Josh stopped by the time we reached my bedroom. As we settled ourselves, Jessi and Mallory ran in.

"Claudia, how did your meeting go?" Jessi asked.

"Well," I began, "the good news is — "

"Listen up, everybody!" Kristy said, her finger poised over my answering machine.

The light was blinking with the number four. Kristy pressed the message button.

"Hi, it's me, Jeannie," the first message began.

"And me!" shouted Shira's voice in the background.

"Call us call us call us!" Jeannie continued. "We are *dying* to know what happened."

"Urrrrggllllghh!" Shira shouted.

"That's Shira, dying. Call us right back!"

Giggle, giggle, giggle, *click*.

Message number two was Joanna: "Claudia? Claudia? Are you there? Wow, you're still with Mrs. Hochberger? Or maybe you're out k-i-s-s-i-n-g with King Mark! Just kidding!"

"Puh-leeze," muttered Stacey.

"Hello, this is Mrs. Addison," the tape continued. "Sorry to call so early, but as you know, five-thirty to six is always busy around our house. Please call me back as soon as possible. I'd like to speak to you about a special assignment. It's K-L-five-three-four-oh-two. Thank you."

"Uh-oh," Stacey said.

"Eeeeeeee!" began the last message. "We're still dying! Call us!"

Mary Anne walked in, looking dismayed. "Who's that?" she asked.

I laughed. "Shira. The girl is crazed."

"Immature is the word," Stacey remarked.

"They are totally obsessed with you," Abby added.

"They're my friends," I said.

"Well, would you ask your friends not to clog up the club phone around meeting time?" Kristy asked. "What if other clients were trying to reach us?"

"Kristy, it does happen to be my phone," I retorted. "And they're not immature, Stacey. They're just excited — "

"I hereby call this meeting to order!" Kristy announced.

"Anyway," I went on, "Mrs. Hochberger thought the idea was — "

"Okay, first order of business," Kristy interrupted, "is the Addisons!"

As she picked up the phone and began tapping out the Addisons' number, I tried again: "The problem is my King, this guy named Mark. He's like, the jerk of the century — "

"Sshhh!" said Kristy. "Hello, Mrs. Addison, it's BSC president Thomas . . . mm-hm . . . all right . . . I understand. Good-bye."

When she hung up, Abby burst out laughing. *"President Thomas?"*

"It sounds more prestigious," Kristy explained. "Anyway, Mrs. Addison says she made a deal with Sean. For this Thursday, when it's Abby's turn, Sean will be called a cositter."

Abby was turning three shades of green. "Uh-oh . . ."

"All it means is that we'll be *sitting* for Corrie but *supervising* Sean," Kristy continued.

"Which means sitting for both of them but making Sean feel important," was Jessi's analysis.

"All right," Abby said. "But I demand a police escort."

"Don't worry," Kristy reassured her. "He's not *that* bad."

"Okay," I barged on, "so Mark is giving Mrs. Hochberger a hard time about my new plan — "

"Who's Mark?" asked Kristy.

"My King!" I replied. "Mark Jaffe."

"I know who that is," Stacey said. "He's cute."

"Wait. This is the little dude we saw outside?" Abby asked.

"That's Josh. Anyway, Mark's lazy. I just know he's not going to do any work on the Royal Service Plan — that's what Josh calls it — "

81

"Just bop him over the head," Abby suggested. "Mark, not Josh. I mean, he's only in seventh grade — "

"Hrrrmph," Mallory said. "Watch it."

"Resign," Kristy suggested. "I mean, why do all the work? It's not even your grade, really."

"It is so!" I protested.

"Oops, I forgot," Kristy said with a grin.

"Don't forget the time commitment," Mary Anne added. "Between homework and sitting — "

"I can do it," I insisted. "Homework doesn't take me as long as it used to. I just need to figure out what to do about Mark — "

"You'll figure out something, I'm sure," Abby said.

"He's probably acting that way because he likes you," Stacey suggested.

That made me laugh. "Right. And the moon is made of cheese."

"It is?" asked Abby.

Kristy rolled her eyes. "Okay, any other business?"

I sighed. Out of the corner of my eye, a Chips Ahoy box winked at me from behind my bedstand.

I reached down to get it.

Nothing like chocolate chip cookies when you're feeling ignored.

CHAPTER 9

Thursday

I was not scared
of Sean. Not Abby
the Lionhearted.

I knew what to do.
Keep an ear out for
him. Answer his
questions. Period.
I was determined
to let him feel inde-
pendent. Unsupervised.

I think it worked
out too well . . .

"Remember, call him a *co-sitter*," Mrs. Addison said.

"Right," Abby agreed.

"We're hoping he'll take some responsibility for his sister," Mr. Addison added.

"Of course," Abby said.

"After he finishes his homework, he can do whatever he wants," Mrs. Addison went on. "He may leave the yard to go to a friend's, but only if he checks with you and promises to be home by dinnertime. That's when we'll be back."

Abby nodded. "You bet."

"Let us know how this works," Mrs. Addison said.

Mr. Addison chuckled. "Who knows? Someday soon you may be taking him into your club."

"Fat chance." (Don't worry, Abby didn't really say that. She caught the words just before they flew out of her mouth.)

After the Addisons left, Abby bounded into the kitchen. There, Corrie was eating a bowl of cereal.

"Breakfast food?" Abby asked.

"I wook oo," said Corrie with a full mouth.

Sean stormed into the kitchen from the direction of the den. "Who said you could eat that?"

Corrie swallowed. "Me."

Sean grabbed the box away.

"Hey!" Corrie screamed, clutching her bowl.

"You know Mom and Dad don't like us to have sugary snacks," Sean scolded her.

"Can I, Abby?" Corrie asked.

"Well, uh, what do you think, Sean?" spoke Abby the Peacemaker. "I guess we can let her finish, but no more food until dinner, huh?"

"All right," Sean replied, walking back to the den. "Keep an eye on her, and let me know if she sneaks anything."

"You're not my sitter, Sean!" Corrie protested.

"Oh, yes, I am!" Sean snapped back. "Co-sitter."

Corrie gave Abby a desperate look. "Is he?"

Abby shrugged. "It's true."

"But that doesn't make sense!" Corrie said. "Why do I need two sitters?"

"It's kind of an audition," Abby said.

"Does that mean he might be my only sitter someday? I'd rather die!"

"We can arrange that!" Sean called out.

"Sean, you disgusting — "

"Uhh, do you have a lot of homework today?" Abby quickly asked.

"English," Corrie grumbled. "Can you test me on vocabulary words?"

"Sure!"

Corrie wolfed down her cereal and headed for the stairs.

On her way after Corrie, Abby peeked into the den. Sean was lying on the couch, reading a book. A spiral notebook lay flat on his chest.

"Is she giving you any trouble?" he asked.

Abby winked. "Everything is under control."

"Good work."

Walking upstairs, Abby couldn't help smiling. This wasn't exactly easy, but she had a feeling it was going to work out.

She sat on Corrie's carpet, keeping the door open to listen for Sean.

"I am the best speller in my grade," Corrie announced, handing Abby a vocabulary sheet. "Read these and ask me to spell them and give a definition."

Abby picked a word from the list. "Paraphernalia."

Corrie's face went blank. "Wait. Can I see that one more time?"

Well, Corrie's spelling was not all it was cracked up to be. (I don't blame her. My mind short-circuits when a word has more than four letters.) Abby had to work pretty hard with her.

Afterward, as Corrie was opening her math book, Abby said, "Your brother's awfully quiet."

"He's probably asleep," Corrie replied. "He

shouldn't be doing his homework on the sofa. You should pour some ice water on him."

Abby stood up. "Be right back."

She tiptoed downstairs and looked into the den. Sean's books were lying on the coffee table, but he wasn't there.

"Sean?" she called out.

Abby walked through the kitchen and into the living room. No Sean. She checked the basement, then went out the back door. It was growing dark outside, and Abby had to hug herself against the cold. *"Sean?"* she shouted as she walked around to the front of the house.

Next door, a stern-faced older man pushed open the front door. "Sean walked that way," he said, pointing up the street.

"Did he say where he was going?" Abby asked.

The man shrugged. "Just saw him through the window. Thought it was strange that he would be going off by himself so late."

"Oh my lord," Abby said under her breath.

The man was glaring at her. "In my day, you could do that. Not anymore. These days it's dangerous."

Abby darted back into the house. "Corrie, put your coat on! We're leaving!"

Corrie came running downstairs. "What happened?"

Abby grabbed her coat from the back of a

kitchen chair. "We have to find your brother. Hurry up!"

Corrie ran into the coat vestibule as Abby headed for the front door.

Suddenly Abby remembered the book Sean had been reading. *My Side of the Mountain.* About a boy who ran away from home to live in the woods.

Her heart sank. That's why Sean didn't want a sitter. He wanted to be free to run away. This was his new way of dealing with his anger. Right this minute he was picking berries. Making fishhooks out of twigs. Hiding in the hollow of a tree.

Abby could see the headlines: BABY-SITTER NEGLECTS TEN-YEAR-OLD BOY. THREE-STATE HUNT UNDER WAY. "I WAS ONLY TRYING TO GIVE HIM FREEDOM," INCOMPETENT SITTER CLAIMS.

"Where are we going?" Corrie said, running out the front door after Abby.

Abby stopped. "He went off to the right. Are there woods over there?"

"Woods?"

Rrrring!

At the sound of the phone, Corrie shouted, "It's him!"

Abby lunged for the door. "Auggh! It's locked!"

"Did you lock the back?" Corrie asked.

Abby was already running.

Rrrring!

"Don't hang up!" Abby yelled.

The back door was open. Abby ran in, dived across the kitchen, and grabbed the receiver.

"Hello?" she said.

"Hello," a voice replied, "this is Connecticut Cable, with a special, limited-time-only installation offer — "

"Sorry! Can't! 'Bye!" Abby stammered.

"I'm sure if you heard the details," the voice persisted, "you'd — " *Boooop!*

Call-waiting!

Abby almost shrieked. She clicked the receiver hook and said, "Call back later! This is an emergency — "

"Abby?"

The voice was unmistakable.

"Sean? Are you all right?"

"Um, do you have nine dollars and fourteen cents?"

"Where are you?"

"At the supermarket — you know, the one at the little mall? I was going to buy some steak for dinner, but I forgot to bring enough money."

Abby didn't know whether to laugh or cry. "Don't move. We're on our way." She slammed the receiver down.

"Where is he?" Corrie demanded.

"Aisle four," Abby replied, barging out the back door.

The strip mall is an old-fashioned, open-air cluster of stores near the Addisons' house. Abby and Corrie sprinted all the way there.

They found Sean sitting on the curb in front of the supermarket.

"Sean, you know you aren't allowed to leave the house without telling me first!" Abby scolded.

"Sorry," Sean said sheepishly. "I was just trying to help."

Abby sighed and sat next to him. "You know I'll have to tell your parents about this. And I'll probably get into trouble too — "

Sean's eyes were focused on a red minivan that was pulling into the lot. "Go! Go away!" he said suddenly.

"Don't you tell me to — " Abby began.

But Sean bolted up and ran.

"Sean, where are you going?" Abby cried out.

Abby and Corrie ran after him. They found him hunched behind a hedge, peering over toward the parking lot.

"You are so weird, Sean," Corrie said. "What about the meat?"

"I wasn't going to go in there with *her*," Sean said, gesturing to Abby.

Abby was looking at the minivan. A tough-looking blond kid about Sean's age stepped out with his dad.

"Is that one of the kids who teases you about having a baby-sitter?" Abby asked.

Sean just glowered at her. "I don't have baby-sitters anymore, remember?" With that, he turned and walked toward home. "And don't walk next to me, okay? Just stay, like, a half block away."

Oh, brother.

Abby and Corrie exchanged a look. They followed precisely a half block behind.

Abby was good and angry. But she saved the fireworks until they arrived home.

Sean was going to have to explain a lot to his parents.

CHAPTER 10

"He's seven minutes late," Mrs. Hochberger said, looking at the clock on her classroom wall.

It was Monday, after school. The buses had already left, and the building was practically empty.

We were supposed to be meeting to discuss how to organize our committees. Volunteer sheets had been posted on the school bulletin board since Tuesday, almost a week before. Today was the deadline for sign-ups.

I had reminded Mark twice about the meeting. But was he there? Noooo.

"Maybe he forgot," I suggested.

Mrs. Hochberger sighed. "Well, I suppose I should take down the sheets now. I'll make copies of them in the office. If he's not here when I'm back, we can start without him."

She stood up and trudged into the hallway.

I took out some homework to pass the time. I

vowed to finish my math by the time Mrs. Hochberger returned.

"AAAAAAARRRGHHHH!"

I was nearly done when a scream made me jump out of my seat.

Mark was standing in the doorway, stretching. The scream? A big, phony yawn.

"Do you *mind?*" I asked.

"Do I mind what?" Mark said.

"If you're going to show up late, the least you can do is not scare me to death."

That familiar dumb, conceited smirk crept across his face like a fungus. "When I'm tired, I yawn," Mark said with a shrug. "Don't you?"

Mrs. Hochberger bustled in with a handful of papers. "Nice of you to come, Your Majesty!" she said cheerfully. "Looks like your idea worked."

She gave both of us copies of the six sign-up sheets, labeled DECORATION, FOOD, PUBLICITY, MUSIC, CHARITY DRIVE, and AWARDS. Each one was covered with names.

"Great!" I exclaimed.

"*Six?*" Mark said. "We have to make six committees?"

"Mark, we've been talking about this," I reminded him. "And the sheets have been up there for days!"

"Okay, okay. I guess I just didn't count," Mark replied.

Mrs. Hochberger smiled patiently and said, "I suggest you call a grand meeting of all committees. Appoint a head for each one, who will report to you regularly. This way, you'll be busy, but you won't be stuck doing all the work."

I nodded. "You can oversee the food committee, Mark, and I'll — "

"Food? Me?" Mark said.

"You *did* talk to your dad about this, right?" I asked.

"Uh . . . yes. I mean, we didn't actually *talk*, but I mentioned it. I think."

Oh, brother.

I glanced at him. He brushed a lock of hair away from his eyes and shrugged.

What did girls see in this guy, anyway?

"I definitely want to oversee the decorations committee," I went on. "We can split the others."

"I'm already doing food," Mark said. "How many others am I supposed to do?"

I shrugged. "How about half?"

"How can I do half a committee?"

"She means split the work evenly," Mrs. Hochberger said.

"I can do, say, the awards and music," I explained. "You do the publicity and charity."

Mark was shaking his head. "I'll be music. You're charity."

"Fine," I said.

"I'll make an announcement tomorrow about the first big committee meeting," Mrs. Hochberger said. "Just name a date. The prom's a week from Saturday, so the sooner the better."

"How about Wednesday, after school?" I said.

"Do I have to be there?" Mark asked.

"Of course you do!" I snapped. "You're the King, in case you forgot!"

"Hey, chill out, Claudia," Mark said. "I thought maybe we could, you know, split the meetings too."

Oh! I felt like screaming at him. Taking his head off. As I glared his way, I could barely unclench my teeth.

His dark eyebrows were upraised. He was meeting my stare without the tiniest flinch. And he was smiling. A let's-keep-our-sense-of-humor smile.

Sigh. I did know what girls saw in him. How could you yell at a face like that?

Arghhh.

"No one says chill out anymore," I grumbled, looking away.

Mrs. Hochberger was smiling at us. When I caught her glance, she dropped her eyes toward a clipboard on her desk. "Okay, you'll want the committees to start working by the weekend at the latest. I can probably arrange access to the gym on Saturday, if you need it."

Mark looked as if he'd just been sentenced to jail. "Whoa, wait a minute. Not Saturday!"

"Sunday, then?" Mrs. Hochberger asked.

"School is for school days," proclaimed King Mark. "Weekends are for relaxing."

I wanted to throttle him again. "Mark, why don't you just drop out? Give someone else a chance to be King. Someone who really cares about the prom."

"Uh, we could do Wednesday instead," Mrs. Hochberger quickly suggested.

"You won't be spoiling your weekends forever, Mark," I barreled ahead. "This is short-term. If you can't be a little flexible, we might as well both give it up and go back to the old tradition."

"Okay, okay," Mark said with a laugh.

I have seen lots of smiles in my life. But honestly, I've never met anyone who had so many different kinds. Mark — lazy, inconsiderate, major pain Mark — was giving me a new one.

What was going on?

"You're right, Claudia," he said. "Saturday's fine."

"So's Wednesday, I guess," I grumbled.

Mrs. Hochberger smiled wearily. "You know, guys, the old way *was* a lot easier."

* * *

Yes, I gave in. The session would be on Wednesday.

I felt so frustrated and confused after the meeting. As I left school, I passed Jennifer and Loretta waiting on the steps.

Just who I wanted to see. The King's groupies.

"Where's Mark?" Loretta asked.

"Inside," I snapped, walking past them.

I was dying to know exactly who had signed up, so I took out my copies of the lists. I almost ran into a tree as I read them.

Josh had signed up for every committee. Jeannie was on the music list, Shira chose the charity committee, and Joanna wanted to do publicity. (I also spotted "Santa Claus" under awards, "E. Presley" under music, and "Ronald McDonald" under food, but they were all in Josh's handwriting.)

I smiled. Maybe this would be fun, despite the King of Creeps.

I thought about decorations. A March prom was unusual. We needed to do something different. Maybe a lion-and-lamb motif.

That was it. Half the gym would be gentle, green, springlike. The other half would be wintry.

On the lamb half, I pictured large, floating clouds of cotton batting. Spring flowers on every table. Vines crawling up the basketball backboards. On the lion half, snow people on the tables. Maybe an ice sculpture.

Sketches. That's what I needed.

I raced home and darted up to my room.

My answering machine was blinking with a four. I grabbed a sketch pad, flopped down onto my bed, and hit the message button.

Message one was a whiny, unfamiliar voice: "Oh, excuse me, wrong number. I was trying to reach the mayor of Stoneybrook."

Message two was someone with a weird foreign accent: " 'Allo? Zee may-ore is not zair? I weel try latair!"

How strange. Had my phone line been crossed with the town hall?

Message three: "Hello, this is Mr. Addison, regarding Thursday's sitting job. Our meeting has been changed to next Monday. I know it's short notice, but please call us back as soon as possible."

CALL ADDISONS, I wrote on the bottom of my sketch pad, as the last message sounded:

"Uh, hello. This is the mayor of Stoneybrook. Have there been any calls for me?"

That voice I recognized.

I burst out laughing. "JO-O-O-OSH!"

What a goon. He'd really fooled me.

My door opened. It was my genius sister, Janine. "Could you keep it down to a dull roar, please?"

"Sorry," I said.

(I ask you, what other high school–age sister in the world makes dumb jokes like that?)

Janine walked back to her room. I picked up my charcoal pencil and sketched out a rough scheme of the SMS gym.

When I heard Janine's door click shut, I played Josh's messages again.

I chuckled to myself. Every last bit of anger and frustration — zip, out the window. What was I worried about? I was the Queen of the Seventh Grade. I was about to pull together the best seventh-grade prom SMS had ever seen. I was a Baby-sitters Club member. And I had good friends who knew how to make me laugh.

I was pretty lucky.

Who cared about Mark Jaffe, anyway?

CHAPTER 11

It was a week of phone tag with the Addisons. During Monday's meeting, we left a message on their answering machine, saying that Stacey was available to baby-sit. On Tuesday, I came home from school to a message from Mrs. Addison, which said, "Not to worry, girls. We have made another arrangement for next Monday evening."

Which was kind of odd. I mean, who was worried? (Well, maybe Mary Anne. She still didn't want to go near the Addisons.)

Anyway, Sean and Corrie were not exactly my number-one concern. Not when I had the Royal Service Plan to worry about.

I was a little nervous at Wednesday's big committee meeting. Mrs. Hochberger had warned us: Expect only about half of the people who signed up. People love to sign, she explained, but they don't follow through.

Well, she was wrong. Way wrong. By the

start of the meeting, her classroom was full.

Except for one crucial person. Yes, King Mark the Lazy was not there. I half expected him to have skipped town. We waited ten minutes and then started without him. Jennifer and Loretta, who were on the music committee, did not look happy.

Can you guess what happened when Mark finally shuffled in twenty minutes late? A round of loud boos? A barrage of spitballs?

No. Practically the whole room burst into applause. *Applause!* A group of boys in back began punching the air and hooting. Loretta and Jennifer discovered their smiles again. Mark took about a dozen bows, grinning as if he'd just won a gold medal at the Olympics.

I wanted to barf.

"Don't worry, Mark, we'll give you a map for next time!" Josh called out.

Mark's face went blank. A whole bunch of people giggled.

Good old Josh. I couldn't help laughing.

But you know the weird thing? Part of me wanted to defend Mark. Partial insanity, I guess. I quickly rejected *that* idea.

Anyway, after that glorious entrance, we plunged right back into work. Two of my friends became committee heads: Joanna for publicity and Josh for awards. Shira was on the charity drive committee, which pleased her mom, I'm sure. (Jeannie had signed up for Mark's music committee, which was now headed by a friend of his named Spud.)

Afterward I practically floated home for the BSC meeting. It was happening. The Royal Service Plan — *my* idea — was under way!

I was singing when Kristy and Abby arrived at 5:25.

"You're in a good mood," Abby remarked. "What happened, you found a good deal on a carton of Snickers?"

Kristy grinned. "Nahhh, her boyfriend walked her home."

"Boyfriend?" I repeated.

Kristy settled herself in the director's chair. "You know, the cute little dude with the hat."

"Josh?" I said. "Look, Kristy, first of all, he's only a year younger than we are. Second, he's not my boyfriend."

"Claudia has a boyfriend?" asked Stacey, rushing through the door. "I want all the dirt."

"Josh," Abby said.

Stacey grinned. "You mean the chipmunk?"

"Will you guys stop it?" I demanded. "He's not a chipmunk, he's not a little dude. He's a friend, with a nice personality and a great sense of humor. That's it."

"What more could you ask for?" Abby commented.

"Touchy, touchy," Kristy said.

"I think the King is much cuter, anyway," Stacey said. "Ask him to call me when he's in eighth grade."

They all burst out giggling.

My terrific mood was going *ffsssssssshhh*, like air from a balloon. I could not believe how superior they were acting. As if I were in kindergarten.

My so-called best friends. Not one of them had asked about the RSP (Royal Service Plan, as you probably figured out).

"You know," I began, "if you would stop joking for a minute, I could tell you — "

"Claudia! How did it go?"

Jessi and Mallory raced into the room, all excited.

"Did the jerk show up?" Jessi asked.

"Did you decide how you're going to decorate the gym?" Mallory asked.

Hallelujah. At least some of my friends cared.

The next day in school, I realized my transformation was complete. In a few short weeks, I had gone from Claudia Who? to Claudia the Human Magnet. Between classes, I could barely walk down the hallway without being stopped by classmates. Questions, questions, questions. How many tables did we need for the charity clothing drive? How can we place

103

an ad on the local radio station, WSTO? Do we need to give awards to everyone, to be fair? How long should the music cassette be?

I gently reminded the people on Mark's committees that they needed to report to him. He usually sent them back to me. (Grrrr.)

I saw Jeannie in the hallway after last period. She looked upset.

"I hate him," she growled.

"Who?" I asked.

"Spud. The head of the music committee. All he likes is fifties, fifties, fifties. We're going to listen to Elvis Presley until we drop."

"We don't have to, Jeannie. You guys are a committee. You're supposed to discuss things."

"That's what I said. You know what Spud answered? 'I'm acting under the King's orders!' "

"Stand up to him, Jeannie!"

"Have you seen how big he is, Claudia? Everyone's afraid of him."

"I'll mention something to Mrs. Hochberger."

We turned into the lobby and walked outside. In front of the school, a group of seventh-graders shouted hello.

I recognized them right away. The food committee. They were supposed to go to Mr. Jaffe's restaurant.

"Where's Mark?" I asked.

"You mean he isn't with you?" asked Loretta, who was the committee head.

Uh-oh.

"I'll be right back," I said.

By then I knew Mark's schedule. He had gym last period, like I did.

I ran toward the boys' locker room. I found Mark sauntering up the hallway, surrounded by adoring classmates.

"Heyyy," he said, flashing his killer smile. "My Queen arriveth!"

Oooh, why why *why* was that smile getting to me? "Hi," I said calmly. "Do you know your committee is waiting out front for you?"

"Committee?" Mark repeated.

"The food committee," I reminded him. "Remember? You're supposed to take them to your dad's restaurant?"

Mark slapped his forehead. "Auuugh! I forgot!"

His friends started laughing. "The Space King," one of them said.

"Daffy Jaffe," remarked another.

"Look, you guys go ahead to Brenner Field," Mark said. "If I have time, I'll meet you later."

As his friends walked away, grumbling, Mark gave me a sheepish look. "We were going to play Ultimate Frisbee. Good thing you caught us."

I heard loud kissing noises from the direction of Mark's friends. One of them had wrapped his arms around himself so that it looked as if someone were hugging him.

The others were cracking up, as if that were the funniest and most original joke ever invented.

"Just ignore those bozos," Mark said, his face turning red.

"It's okay." Part of me wanted to laugh. But I was still upset about the food committee. I looked toward the front door. "So — ?"

"Don't worry, I'll take care of them," Mark quickly said. He took a deep breath and began walking. "My dad may pin me with the meat cleaver, but hey, a king has to take risks, right?"

I watched him go. I didn't know what to say. As he disappeared around the corner, I called out, "Good luck, King Mark."

He'd probably need it.

CHAPTER 12

Monday

I wasn't supposed to be writing
in this. My job at the Addisons'
was canceled for today. They'd
made other arrangements. At
least that's what their message
said last week.

Well, you'll never guess who made
those arrangements . . .

It all started at approximately 5:35. The Monday BSC meeting had just begun, and I was about to unload all my complaints about Mark.

The ring of the telephone cut me off.

I snatched up the receiver. "Hello, Babysitters Club. Queen Claudia speaking."

I was just kidding around. I like to see how grown-ups react to silly greetings.

But the answer was not silly.

Nor was it from a grown-up.

"Hello? Claudia? It's — it's — OWWW!"

I heard a loud crash. Then the clunk of a dropped telephone. "Hello?" I repeated. "Hello?"

More crashing and thumping. Then, "It's Sean! Can someone come over? Not a sitter, but you know, someone to help me?"

"Sean, what's wrong?" I cried.

"I'm alone and — well, I kind of had an accident — a really bad one!"

"Are you all right? Is it something serious?"

"Uh, I have to go! Come over now!"

The line went dead. I hung up. "Sean's in trouble. He's all alone in the house."

"*Alone?*" Mary Anne said. "I thought they had a sitter!"

Stacey was already putting on her coat. "It was my job. I'll go."

"Can someone drive her?" Kristy asked.

"My parents are still at work," I replied.

Stacey zoomed out before we could say good-bye.

The Addisons live at least a half mile from my house, but Stacey ran all the way there.

From outside, the house looked fine. At least it wasn't a fire, Stacey thought.

She sprinted up the front porch steps, rang the bell, and banged on the door.

The door flew open. Sean's face was red and tear-streaked. "I — I didn't mean — in the kitchen — " he stammered.

"Where's Corrie?" Stacey demanded.

"At a friend's house," Sean replied. "Play-ing."

Stacey bolted inside. She raced through the dining room and into the kitchen.

And then she saw what had happened.

Bubbles.

Mounds of them. Billowing out of the dish-washer and all over the floor, practically bury-ing the legs of the kitchen table and chairs.

"Oh my lord," Stacey murmured.

"I didn't mean to do it!" Sean blurted out. "I was just trying to do the dishes!"

The dishwasher was completely buried un-der the suds, but Stacey could hear it chugging away. She plunged into the mess, bushwhack-ing through the bubbles. When she uncovered the control panel, she pressed the off switch.

"Help me beat them down!" Stacey commanded, swinging her arms through the mess.

With grim determination, Stacey and Sean stamped, swatted, and blew on the suds, trying desperately to make the pile manageable.

I wish I could have been there. I would have been hysterical.

Stacey and Sean were not seeing the humor of it, though. Sean was practically in tears.

"How did you do this, Sean?" Stacey asked.

"I don't know!" Sean replied. "I just put in the detergent, closed the door, and pressed the — "

"What detergent?" Stacey asked.

Sean pointed to the dishwashing liquid by the sink. "That."

Stacey groaned. "No wonder! You're supposed to use dishwashing detergent!"

"Well, you wash dishes with that stuff, don't you?"

"Dishes in the sink, not dishes in the dishwasher! It's different."

"Why?"

"Never mind. Just help me clean up."

Stacey tossed him a sponge. She filled the bucket with water from the tap and went to work with the mop.

They both scrubbed away. When the floor was clean, Stacey dumped the suds into the sink and noticed that the Addisons have an old-fashioned hose attachment near the sink faucet. Stacey used it to spray down the suds inside the dishwasher.

The spraying left a pool of frothy water at the bottom, below the plate rack.

"What now?" Sean asked.

Stacey shrugged. She closed the dishwasher door and scanned the control panel. "Maybe this'll do it," she said, pressing Cancel.

Sure enough, the Cancel button drained out the water. But it also made a few more bubbles that spilled out the edges of the door.

Stacey had to spray the bubbles and run Cancel about four times before the mess was totally cleaned up. Finally she poured in some real dishwashing detergent and let the machine run its normal cycle.

She and Sean plopped themselves down on the kitchen chairs.

"I'm sorry, Stacey," Sean whimpered. "Now I'll know better."

"Sean, why are you here alone, anyway?" Stacey asked. "Where's your baby-sitter?"

Sean was looking at the floor. "I'm the sitter."

"*You?* Your mom said she'd made arrangements."

"She did. With me," Sean mumbled. "I told her none of the Baby-sitters Club sitters could make it."

"But we called you! We left a message that said I was coming!"

Sean didn't speak for a long time. When he did, his voice was barely audible. "My mom and dad let me take down the messages on the phone machine. I write them on a sheet of paper. Anyway, I heard the message from the Baby-sitters Club, and, well, I changed it."

"You lied?" Stacey interpreted. "You purposely gave your parents the wrong message?"

Sean nodded. "I wanted to prove I don't need a sitter. I told them I could stay home by myself with the doors locked. It was just me. I wasn't going to have to take care of Corrie. I said they could call me as much as they wanted, to check up. And I wanted to surprise them with clean dishes when they came home."

Stacey sighed deeply. "You are going to have a lot to explain to your parents."

"But — but it was just a mistake!" Sean insisted.

"Look, Sean. If your parents decide you don't need a sitter, fine. But they didn't decide that. You forced them into this by lying. And look what happened. At this rate, I wouldn't be surprised if you have to take a sitter to college with you!"

Sean's bottom lip quivered. He ran out of the kitchen and into the den, sobbing.

Stacey felt a pang of guilt. She followed after him.

He was curled up on a sofa, hiding his face behind a throw pillow.

"I'm sorry," Stacey said. "I didn't mean that last part."

"You're right!" came Sean's muffled voice from behind the pillow. "I'm nothing but a big baby! I can't do anything!"

"That's not true."

"Yes, it is! You should buy me a pacifier and walk me to school every day!"

"Sean . . ."

"Other kids in my grade can stay home by themselves. But me? No!"

"What other kids?" Stacey asked.

Sean sat up and threw the pillow aside. "Like Mel Tucker! He hasn't had a sitter since he was nine!"

A blond, tough-looking boy. That was Abby's description of the boy Sean had run away from in the mall parking lot. Abby didn't know Mel Tucker, but Stacey did. And the description fit.

"Sean, is *Mel* the guy who's been giving you trouble in school?" Stacey asked.

Sean nodded.

"I know him," Stacey said. "He lives near the Hobarts."

"Have you baby-sat for him?" Sean asked.

"No, but — "

"See?"

"Sean, we are not the only baby-sitters in town," Stacey said. She remembered seeing Mel with a girl, about high school age, at the supermarket.

Stacey found the local phone book and set it on the kitchen desk. "If there's another extension of the phone, go to it."

As Sean ran off, Stacey looked up Tucker and tapped out the number.

"I'm here," said Sean from the other line.

Stacey shushed him. The line rang twice and a deep male voice said, "Frank Tucker here."

"Hello, Mr. Tucker, I'm Stacey McGill, calling on behalf of the Baby-sitters Club. I was wondering if you might need our services for your children?"

"I only have one child," Mr. Tucker said with a chuckle. "And we have a regular sitter, my niece who lives nearby. She and Melvin are very close. But thanks anyway."

"Thank *you*," Stacey said. "Good-bye."

Stacey waited for Sean triumphantly at the bottom of the stairs. As he thumped down, she folded her arms. "Well, what do you have to say now?"

Sean's face was lit up with a big, sly grin.

"His name is *Melvin*?"

* * *

By the time the Addisons arrived home with Corrie, Sean and Stacey had both calmed down. Of course, the Addisons were puzzled to see her. She began to explain, but Sean stopped her.

"I did it," he said softly. "So I guess I should be the one to explain."

Stacey stayed while Sean told them everything — the lie, the dishwasher, the call to the BSC. The Addisons listened intently. They did not look happy.

Stacey slipped out while they were discussing a suitable punishment.

She hoped they wouldn't go overboard. She knew Sean had learned his lesson.

In fact, she was kind of proud of him. He might prove to be baby-sitter material yet.

CHAPTER 13

"SHAMALAMALAMA, SHOOP-BOP SHA-BING-BONG!"

I don't know about you, but I am not a big fan of fifties music.

Especially loud fifties music, blaring out of speakers while I'm supposed to be helping the decoration and music committees set up the gym.

That's where I was on the Friday before the seventh-grade prom. I was standing on a ladder, stringing a plastic vine through a basketball net. The speakers were against the wall, about ten feet away. *"Will someone lower that?"* I shouted.

Good old Spud was at the amplifier. "Sorry!" he said, turning down the volume knob.

"Are we going to hear anything good?" I asked.

"Don't worry," Jeannie called from across the room. "We made him mix in some real music."

"Thank you!"

Boy, was my temper short. I felt totally fried.

All week long, my Royal Service Plan had been on the verge of collapse.

Black Tuesday almost destroyed us. First the King and Queen capes came back from the dry cleaners, ripped to shreds. Mrs. Hochberger told us the school budget had no money for new ones.

That same day, Spud threw a tantrum when Jeannie asked him to include non-fifties music. And Joanna realized all the publicity notices she'd posted around town had contained the wrong date.

As for Mark? Well, he announced that he'd quit. I think he was embarrassed about the scene at the Argo.

When that happened, I wanted to throw in the towel myself.

I might have, too, if Josh hadn't given me a "Testimony of Loyalty to the Queen," signed by a bunch of kids and rolled up to look like a scroll.

Then, on Wednesday, Mark bounced into school saying he and his dad had patched things up. Mr. Jaffe would be happy to provide the food *and* the kitchen — for a fraction of what it would cost to cater the prom. With the extra money, Mrs. Hochberger was able to buy brand-new capes. And Joanna managed to replace all the fliers with corrected ones. She'd thought of a great name, too — "Lion to Lamb Seventh-Grade Jam."

Mark really started to shape up after his father's decision. At least he seemed to. I saw him talking to food committee members in the hallways a lot, and I even saw him deep in conversation with Mrs. Hochberger once or twice.

I didn't have a chance to talk to him, though. I was busy myself. I have to admit, even though I was only supposed to be supervisor to the decorations committee, I kind of went overboard. I helped decide on the materials, went shopping for them after school, and designed a wraparound mural that depicted winter turning to spring. I also helped make the frames for a huge papier-mâché lion and lamb, which the committee was finishing in shop class.

Now, the day before the prom (yikes!), my great dream was taking shape.

Sort of. King Mark was walking around with a clipboard, looking lost.

"Uh, Claudia?" he called, "Mr. Halprin says he can only give us seven long tables."

Turning toward him, I caught my finger in one of the metal hooks on the basketball hoop. "Yeeeouch! Uh, Mark? I'm kind of busy right now."

"Well, seven won't be enough for the food and the clothing drive. I guess I could find some big cardboard boxes — "

"Right, Mark, those'll look just great with our decorations."

"How about if we drape the clothing over the basketball hoops?"

Ooooh. He was annoying me now. Back to his old tricks. I gave him a fierce Look. "Ha ha."

"Hey, just kidding," he said with a grin.

I climbed down the ladder. "Is everything a joke with you?"

"Not everything. You're not."

"What do you mean by that? Do you *like* to make me angry?"

Mark shrugged and looked away. "At least you talk to me."

"What's that supposed to mean?"

"Nothing."

"It doesn't mean *nothing!*"

"Exactly."

"I mean, it means not nothing. Something. You know what I mean."

"I do?"

"Now you're making fun of me!"

That smile. That self-satisfied, I'm-smarter-than-you smile was driving me crazy.

I raised my arms. I don't exactly know what

I was going to do. Pound him on the shoulders? Smack him in the face? Pull my own hair?

I couldn't decide. So I just stood there.

"I hope you're not ticklish," Mark said. "Because you're in a vulnerable position."

We locked eyes. Then I lost it.

A laugh blew out of me. So did a teeny spray of saliva. Mark backed away.

I was out of control. Hysterical. Cracking up. I don't know why. Maybe it was the pressure of the week. Maybe it was Mark's expression. Maybe it was the word *vulnerable*, which sounded so strange coming from him. Maybe it was the ridiculous idea of his tickling me.

Whatever it was, he seemed pretty stunned. His smile wasn't so cocky anymore. It was halfway between amused and confused.

"Claudia? Are you all right?"

He looked so earnest. Like a little boy. That made me crack up even more.

Mrs. Hochberger walked by, smiling and shaking her head. "Uh-oh," she said, "she's losing it."

Mark was trying to laugh with me, but I could tell he wasn't sure why. "Claudia, can I ask you what's so funny?"

"You," I said.

Whoosh. All the tension left his face. "Really? I made you laugh?"

"Pleased with yourself, huh?" I couldn't believe that I, polite Claudia, was talking like this.

"No! I mean, yes. I mean, it's good to make people laugh. I mean, I wasn't trying or anything. But I'm glad. I like it when you laugh."

Mark's face was turning red, even though he looked pretty proud of himself.

Off went the warning bells in my head. The last thing I needed was to boost Mark Jaffe's ego.

"Well, it wasn't really anything you said, just something in my own head," I said, turning toward the ladder. "Anyway, back to work."

When I looked over my shoulder, Mark was off with the music committee. I watched him for awhile. He went straight to the sound system and adjusted levels. He greeted Mr. Halprin and started setting up tables. He even picked up a broom and swept away some streamers that had fallen.

As I climbed the ladder, I noticed Loretta glaring at me.

"Uh-oh," Jeannie muttered from below. "She's jealous."

I gave her a Look. "Oh, puh-*leeze!* Don't make me laugh."

Jeannie shrugged. "You just *were* laughing, Claudia. A lot. With Markie-poo."

"*At* him," I snapped. "Not with him."

"Oh?" Jeannie raised and lowered her eyebrows suggestively.

I had to look away. I would not even dignify that. I was disgusted. Totally disgusted.

I strung the vines carefully, and the hoop now looked totally cool, like a strange tree (with a huge square of glass behind it).

As I descended the ladder, I looked around for a reaction. But everyone seemed too busy to notice.

Except Mark. He was smiling at me. When I caught his glance, he gave me the thumbs-up sign.

I smiled back, but only because I didn't want to be rude. Quickly, too, because I had to deal with the most important part of the prom.

The lion and lamb were being wheeled in on a dolly.

I hadn't seen them since the committee began layering the papier-mâché. And now, as Mr. Halprin swung open a set of double doors, I saw the finished, painted products for the first time. "Ta-da!" shouted my committee head, Bonnie Lasher.

Everyone applauded.

Me? I nearly had a heart attack.

The lion looked like a hyena. He had this stupid smile, with human-movie-star teeth. His mane had been made from scraggly brown yarn that hung limply from his neck. His skin was a mottled yellow, as if he'd fallen asleep in a bed of daffodils.

The lamb was even worse. It had been painted totally white, no detail whatsoever. As if it were wearing a straitjacket. Its eyes were crossed and angry looking, its tail was curly like a pig's, and obviously someone had goofed up on the mouth, because it was a big black blotch.

"Looks good," Jeannie said, patting me on the back.

I somehow managed to unclench my teeth. *"Good?"* I whispered. "You call that good? It looks like a kindergarten art project. They're hideous, Jeannie. They're going to ruin everybody's appetite."

Jeannie chuckled. "You're just being an artist, Claudia."

I wanted to rip the sculptures apart. I wanted to send the committee back — no, fire them and do it all myself.

Calm down, I told myself. They had worked hard. And they were volunteering their time. I could not be ungrateful.

Bonnie raced to me, all excited. "What do you think?"

I forced up the corners of my lips into a smile. It felt like lifting a house. "Stunning."

"Yeeeaaaa!" she shouted in triumph.

The rest of the session? What I remember

most was trying to avoid looking at the animals. Every time I caught a glimpse, I wanted to cry.

I was baffled. Didn't anyone else realize how awful they were? Were they all so ignorant about art? Or was I being too harsh?

I tried to stay positive. I helped Bonnie set up tables. I talked with her about the flower arrangements (her parents were picking them up from a florist two hours before the prom).

I was stringing fake icicles across the winter side of the room when I realized everyone was gone.

Well, everyone except Mark. He was fiddling with the tape player. A soft rock ballad was playing, one that I really liked.

I glanced at my watch.

5:19. Yikes!

I ran toward the gym door. "See you tomorrow, Mark! I have to — "

What came next happened so fast I can barely remember it. I know my foot slipped on a pile of crepe paper. I know I fell. And I know Mark helped me up.

Then we were standing toe to toe. I meant to thank him and race out the door. But I didn't. I was looking in his eyes. And I was noticing the tiny, luminous flecks of light brown in them, almost orange in their dark surroundings.

I wanted to say something, but I couldn't. This was Mark Jaffe, after all.

Mark smiled gently. "Are you hurt?"

"Nuck." My voice caught in my throat, and I swallowed. "No."

I was lying. Something *was* wrong. With my legs, for one thing. They were not moving. With my lungs too. They weren't sending me enough air.

Not to mention my brain. It felt like a big Etch-a-Sketch. On it was a big jagged drawing of my bedroom, with six angry BSC faces. But it was slowly shaking, to the rhythm of the song. And a big color image was replacing the old one. An image of deep brown eyes and a smile that reached inside me to my toes.

What was happening?

I couldn't answer that question. I didn't want to.

I didn't think much at all as Mark moved closer. As he softly pressed his lips to mine.

All I did was close my eyes.

And press back.

CHAPTER 14

"I call this meeting of the Baby-sitters Club to order!" exclaimed Kristy.

What had I done?

"Any new business?"

Out of my mind. I'd been out of my mind. *Mark Jaffe?*

"I have a Sean update."

Okay. Pay attention. Stacey. That was Stacey.

I was trying to keep track of the meeting. But it wasn't easy. I felt as if I were in a bubble, floating outside my room. Upside down.

My life had turned completely upside down.

From head to toe, I was charged. As if I'd put my finger into an electrical socket and hadn't quite recovered. Something must have been wrong with my mouth nerves. First my lips would feel as if they were asleep, then they'd feel all tingly and swollen. I kept needing to touch them, I don't know why.

"He was all smiles when I saw him yesterday. Seems he saw Mel and Tootsie Roll to blabberjabber ragweed . . ."

Well, something like that. I couldn't really tell. Everything around me — the words, the faces — all of it was fading in and out. I had no idea what was going on.

Had it really happened? Could I really have kissed Mark Jaffe?

Impossible.

Totally absurd.

It had to be a nightmare.

But I didn't feel scared. I didn't feel disgusted. I was thinking of Mark's face, and all I could do was smile!

"Claudia?"

The pressure was making me crack. That had to be it.

"Earth to Claudia!"

"Huh?"

Plop. I fell out of my bubble. Six perplexed faces were staring at me.

"Have you been listening?" Kristy asked.

"Sure, sure," I replied.

"Then, what did Stacey just say?"

"Um, about Sean," I tried. "He's better."

Stacey gave an exasperated sigh. "When Mel started teasing him, Sean calmly mentioned that he knew about Mel's baby-sitter. That shut Mel right up. Then Sean took him aside and said, 'Tease me again, Mel*vin,* and everybody finds out. Leave me alone, and it's a secret between me and you.' "

A secret between me and you. That was how it had to be. I had to call Mark. Had to tell him it was all a big mistake. No one — absolutely no one — could find out. "Uh-huh," I muttered.

"Claudia, are you okay?" Mary Anne asked.

"Fine," I shot back.

"She's tired," Jessi said. "She's been working hard all week."

"I knew this would happen," Kristy grumbled.

"How was the setup today?" Mallory asked.

Kristy harrumphed. "Can we finish important business first?"

"This *is* important," Jessi insisted.

"Well," I said, "we steamed the strungers . . . uh, sprung the screamers . . ."

He was telling his friends. I just knew it. He was on the phone, bragging. *I kissed the Queen,* he was saying. *I kissed Claudia Kishi.*

I could not let him do that.

"Uh, would you guys mind waiting downstairs while I make a private phone call?" I asked.

Total silence. I looked around. My friends' faces formed a group Duh.

"This is some kind of a joke, right?" Abby asked.

"Look, it's . . . well, kind of an emergency," I stammered. "A personal one."

"This is club time, Claudia," Kristy reprimanded me. "Not personal time. You know the rules."

"Kristyyy," Jessi said.

"It's important," I insisted.

"How important can it be?" Kristy demanded. "I mean, if it's just some piddly seventh-grade prom stuff — "

"It's not piddly!" I shot back. "What is with you, Kristy? You think seventh grade is so far beneath you? You think I'm hanging around with kids in diapers?"

"Here we go again." Kristy groaned.

"For your information," I said, "one of those cute little kids just kissed me in the gym. When was the last time that happened to you, Kristy Thomas?"

Swallow it, Claudia!

Too late.

"You mean, the little guy?" Abby asked. "Jason?"

"Josh," I corrected her. "And it wasn't him."

"Who was it?" almost all of them asked in unison.

"Marrhaaffi," I mumbled, turning around to reach for a box of Milk Duds behind my bed.

"Who?" the chorus repeated.

I popped in a few Duds. "Markaafffee."

Stacey laughed. "Swallow, please. It sounded like you said Mark Jaffe."

I nodded. "I did."

Their jaws dropped open. If I'd had popcorn, I could have taken some target practice.

"The guy you hate?" Mary Anne asked.

"Well, I didn't mean to. He kissed me. And I — well, I was just kissing back."

"Why didn't you push him away?" Jessi asked.

"I didn't want to," I said. "He was being gentle and nice — "

"Did anyone see?" Mallory asked with a grin.

"I hope not," I said.

"Me too," Kristy replied. "I mean, Claudia, please. He's in seventh grade!"

The Milk Duds flew out of my hands. Kristy had to duck. "Hey!"

"I have had enough!" I said. "Do you think I understand what happened today? No way! I have hated this guy. I'm a wreck."

"Claudia, she's just concerned," Stacey explained. "You know, about his maturity."

"Look, I'm not going to sit here and defend Mark Jaffe," I said. "But for your information, he was left back once, so he is our age."

"We didn't know that!" Abby exclaimed. "Why didn't you say so before?"

"What's the difference?" I said. "I can't believe the way you guys are treating me. I'm not Gulliver in the land of the Lilipulitzers — "

" — putions," Mallory said.

"Gesundheit. When you make fun of seventh-graders, do you ever stop to think how it makes me feel? Not to mention Jessi and Mal? Well, I have news for you. Some of my seventh-grade friends are twice as mature as you. And Mark Jaffe happens to be just as cool as any eighth-grader I know."

There. I'd said it.

But what had I said? I was defending Mark Jaffe. Did I really mean to?

What was happening to me?

I caught Kristy's glance. I thought she was going to scream at me. Kick me out of the club. Toss the phone at my head.

At this point, I didn't really care. I was ready to be treated as an equal, or not treated at all.

Kristy stood up. She turned her back to me and picked up the box of Milk Duds. "Your aim isn't as good as it used to be, Claudia," she said. "Next time, you need to use more wrist action."

Abby burst out laughing.

"Kristy, did you hear what I said?" I demanded.

Kristy's face was red. "Okay, I'm a jerk. I'll admit it."

"Me too, Claud," Stacey said softly. "I didn't mean to be snobby. It's been hard to see you with a new bunch of friends, that's all."

"So you have to make fun of them?" I asked.

"Immature, huh?" Kristy said softly.

"We really miss you in class," Mary Anne spoke up.

"Without you, lunch is boring," Kristy added.

"I'll say," Abby agreed. "We have to listen to Kristy all period."

Now it was Kristy's turn to fling Milk Duds.

I couldn't help laughing. "Apologies accepted, I suppose."

I caught Mary Anne's glance. She started blubbering. I threw my arms around her.

Soon I was surrounded. It felt wonderful.

I didn't bother calling Mark. Whatever happened, happened.

CHAPTER 15

"Here it comes!" Jeannie exclaimed. "We put it on the tape right after this song!"

Josh was fumbling with the clasp on the cape around my neck. "Hold still!" he said.

"Put what on?" I asked Jeannie. " 'Pumpin' Circumstance'?"

"*Pomp*," Jeannie said. " 'Pomp and Circumstance.' "

I could barely hear her. Inside the gym, a loud rock tune was playing over the speakers. The sound carried through the closed side door, and into the hallway.

I was exhausted. I was shaking. I was sweating like a pig. My hair felt like warmed-over linguini. All day long, I'd been running around the school. Helping with the tables, the flowers, the food. Answering questions. Trying to figure out what to say to you-know-who.

Every time I saw Mark, I froze up. I'd try to speak, but my tongue would suddenly feel like a woolen sock and all I could manage was "Hi."

Whenever we did talk to each other, it was about prom setup. I believe I was able to ask "Would you help me move this table?" and "Do we have enough chairs?"

Very romantic.

Now Mark was in the hall on the other side of the gym, waiting. In a few moments, we would make our grand entrances (yes, from two different sides, like a wedding. Is that corny or what?). Eventually we'd have to dance to the official seventh-grade song, called "I Don't Want to Say Good-bye," by the band U4Me.

Whenever that happened, we would be forced to — well, to quote Mrs. Hochberger, "Everyone will want you to kiss, but you are under no obligation."

That's what I was worried about. Kiss number two. I mean, one kiss can always be counted as a mistake. But two? Let's face it, that's a relationship.

How did Mark feel about this? I had no idea. Was he looking forward to another kiss? Was he going to run away, screaming "Cooties"? Was I? Nothing would surprise me.

Ever since I had brought up the subject at the BSC meeting, I'd been listening to advice. Jessi, Mallory, and Mary Anne thought I should

apologize politely and tell him to bug off.
When I mentioned my dilemma to Jeannie,
Joanna, and Shira, they almost barfed. Stacey,
Kristy, and Abby were the only ones who said
"Go for it." I'd been way too embarrassed to
bring up the subject with Josh.

Shira must have been reading my mind. "Remember, Claudia, tell Mark you weren't in
your right mind. You didn't mean it."

"Claudia, don't move!" Josh urged me, still
trying to fasten the clasp. "What didn't you
mean?"

"The kiss," Jeannie replied. "Didn't Claudia
tell you? She and the King lip-wrestled yesterday."

Josh's hand slipped. The clasp pinched my
neck. "Yeow!" I said. "Careful, Josh."

"Oh! Sorry! I — I was just laughing to myself. I mean, the idea of you kissing Mark.
What a joke."

"No joke," Jeannie said.

Joanna shot her a Look. "Can we change the
subject?"

"She washed off the cooties afterward,"
Shira said. "Besides, she didn't mean it. You
know Mark."

Josh was staring at me, totally aghast. "You
mean, he forced you?"

"Go beat him up, Josh!" Jeannie shouted.

"He didn't *force* me," I said.

"You did it on purpose?" Josh asked.

DAAAAAA - DADADAAAA - DAAAAA - DAAAAA . . . blared my entrance music.

"Josh, my cape!" I cried.

Josh's fingers were shaking so much, I had to fasten it myself, blindly. *"I'm* the one who's supposed to be nervous," I said. "Not you."

"Sorry," Josh replied.

"How do I look?" I asked, turning around with a queenly flourish.

"A smile would be nice," Shira replied.

Bing! I was ready for a toothpaste commercial.

Jeannie pulled open the door. "It's show time!"

"Good luck," Josh murmured. He still looked shaky. Boy, was he taking this seriously.

I started to walk. The collar pulled against my throat and I gagged. "Hold the cape!" I gasped.

Jeannie immediately lifted the cape. I was regal again. Now everyone could see my outfit — a frilly Victorian satin dress that I am convinced was donated to the thrift shop by a member of the royal family.

A huge roar of applause went up. I could see Mark on the other side of the room. He was flanked by two friends, wearing long gray wigs and sunglasses (weird).

We both walked onto a platform at one end

136

of the gym. Mark flashed me a great big smile. Well, maybe it wasn't for me, specifically. Maybe he was just happy.

If I hadn't been so obsessed about you-know-what, I'd have been happy too.

When the music stopped, Mrs. Hochberger gave a short speech. Afterward, as we stepped off the platform, Mark said, "Everything looks great."

He was right. The "lamb" side of the gym was green with flowers, the "lion" side wintry but cheerful. Even the two papier-mâché animals didn't seem to look so bad anymore.

When I turned to answer Mark, he was gone. Off to his friends' table. I think Loretta was his date. Or maybe Jennifer. I couldn't tell. They were both sitting at the table. Maybe they were taking shifts.

I made my way to my table and took off my cape. Jeannie, Shira, and Joanna were sitting with their dates, three guys I barely knew.

Josh, technically, was my date. We sat together. We chatted. I helped him organize his awards list. But I couldn't help noticing he wasn't himself. He seemed distracted and distant. I thought at first he was sick, but then I realized he must have been preoccupied with the awards ceremony.

The awards ceremony, by the way, went off with flying colors. Some of Josh's awards were hilarious, like "Most Likely to Eat with His Fingers in a Restaurant" and "Loudest Public Burp of the Year." Others were of the traditional "Most Likely to Succeed" variety. (I received "Queen of All Queens." Good old Josh.)

After the awards, Josh and I danced — one rock tune, followed by a fifties song, followed by a soft ballad. We made sure to make faces at Shira, who was standing behind a table piled with donated goods and trying to smile for a *Stoneybrook News* photographer.

During the first two numbers, Mark sat at his table, surrounded by his admirers. The King holding court. During the ballad, Loretta dragged him onto the dance floor.

She proceeded to yak Mark's ear off. As they swept by, he gave me a Look. A *get-me-out-of-here* Look. I couldn't help giggling.

"What are you staring at?" Josh asked.

"Mark," I said. "He is being funny."

"Mmm-hmm. I guess he's not a big, dumb, rude, conceited jerk, after all."

I shook my head. "Everybody has good points."

Josh smiled faintly. "Doctor Rocker sees zat you haff pairhaps zlight feelinks for zis fellow?" he said in a strange accent.

I laughed. "I guess I'm nervous. The seventh-grade song is coming up soon on the tape. I have to dance with him. I guess we'll have to talk about . . . you know."

"The kiss," Josh said.

"Yeah." I felt myself blushing.

"Well, what do you want to do, Claudia?"

"Do?"

"About Mark. You have to say something. I mean, do you want to go steady with him?"

I wasn't expecting that question. But I had thought about it. "I don't know, Josh. Maybe."

Josh fell silent as the song ended. The next sound I heard was the beginning of "I Don't Want to Say Good-bye," the seventh-grade song. I froze up.

All around the room, eyes were staring at me.

"Ohhhh." I groaned. "This is it."

Josh let go of me. "Well," he said with a gentle smile. "What are you waiting for? Go for it, girl."

I gave him a quick hug. "Josh, you are the *best* friend."

Then I took a deep breath and faced Mark. He was walking toward me with a grin that could have lit up the gym in a power blackout.

"Go! Go! Go! Go!" our classmates were shouting all around us.

"Dance?" Mark asked.

I held out my arms, and we moved to the song.

The room sounded like a bird sanctuary — screeches and whistles and loud hooting.

"Very grown-up, huh?" I said.

The chanting transformed into "Kiss! Kiss! Kiss! Kiss!"

Mark was blushing. "Should we?"

"We've done it before," I replied.

He laughed.

I laughed.

We spun around the gym. I could see Shira, Jeannie, and Joanna. Josh was turning away, ducking into the crowd.

I could see mouths shouting, I could see hands clapping, but I couldn't hear a thing. Only the music and my heart thumping inside me.

And soon I could see only Mark. And I didn't care what anyone was shouting, or who was looking.

Our lips met. For the second time.

No doubt about it now.

It was a relationship.

And it felt very, very good.

Dear Reader,

Claudia is now queen of the seventh grade, but when she was first sent back, she was scared and unhappy. When I started seventh grade, I was nervous, too. All the seventh-graders had moved to Valley Road School from the sixth-grade school, and we were now in junior high. For the first time, we were switching classes all day long and had locker combinations to remember, and the eighth=graders seemed so much older than us! Furthermore, near the beginning of the school year, the entire seventh grade had to go to a camp about an hour away, for three days and three nights. I was terrified. I had never been to camp, and I didn't want to go away with so many people I didn't know. Of course, everything turned out fine, and once we got there we had a good time. My old friends were on the trip, and I made some new ones as well. When it was over and we came home, I couldn't believe I had worried about it so much. Seventh grade turned out to be fine, too. While I was never queen of the seventh grade, my old and new friends and I had a good year.

Happy reading,

Ann M Martin

Ann M. Martin

About the Author

ANN MATTHEWS MARTIN was born on August 12, 1955. She grew up in Princeton, NJ, with her parents and her younger sister, Jane.

Although Ann used to be a teacher and then an editor of children's books, she's now a full-time writer. She gets the ideas for her books from many different places. Some are based on personal experiences. Others are based on childhood memories and feelings. Many are written about contemporary problems or events.

All of Ann's characters, even the members of the Baby-sitters Club, are made up. (So is Stoneybrook.) But many of her characters are based on real people. Sometimes Ann names her characters after people she knows, other times she chooses names she likes.

In addition to the Baby-sitters Club books, Ann Martin has written many other books for children. Her favorite is *Ten Kids, No Pets* because she loves big families and she loves animals. Her favorite Baby-sitters Club book is *Kristy's Big Day*. (By the way, Kristy is her favorite baby-sitter!)

Ann M. Martin now lives in New York with her cats, Gussie and Woody. Her hobbies are reading, sewing, and needlework — especially making clothes for children.

THE BABY-SITTERS CLUB

Notebook Pages

This Baby-sitters Club book belongs to _Crystal_.

I am _10_ years old and in the _4th_ grade.

The name of my school is _Shaffer Elem._

I got this BSC book from _mom_

I started reading it on _march 21_ and finished reading it on _April 25_.

The place where I read most of this book is _When Sean was left alone at home._

My favorite part was when _Cladia and mark Kosse at the danee_

If I could change anything in the story, it might be ~~the part when~~ _that cladia kissed Josh instead mark_

My favorite character in the Baby-sitters Club is _cladia_

The BSC member I am most like is _Cladia_ because _I am a good artist_

If I could write a Baby-sitters Club book it would be about _Cladia and mark_

#106 Claudia, Queen of the Seventh Grade

Claudia is pleased to be chosen Queen of the Seventh Grade.

If I were to choose a King and Queen of my grade, I would

choose ___Katie___ and ___Tyler___

_____, because __They are__

__funny and athletic__ . Once she

is chosen as Queen, Claudia does more than plan the big seventh-

grade dance — she also helps her grade to raise money for

charities. If I were elected Queen or King of my grade, I

would __Buy milk shakes__

__for everyone__

_____. At first, Claudia doesn't like Mark Jaffe, the

King of the Seventh Grade. But then she finds herself kissing

him! This is what I think of Mark Jaffe: __He's a goofball__

__but is nice__ . If I could

decide whether Mark and Claudia stay together or break up, I

would want them to __stay together__

because __they have a lot in__

__common__ .

Finger painting at 3...

A spooky sitting adven

Sitting for two of my favorite charges --
Jamie and Lucy Newton.

SCRAPBOOK

... oil painting
at 13!

my family. Mom and Dad, me and
Janine... and we'll never forget Mimi.

Interior art by Angelo Tillery

Look for #107

MIND YOUR OWN BUSINESS, KRISTY!

The whole thing had blown up in my face.

I should have minded my own business. I should have just left well enough alone and concentrated on running the softball clinic. Even that was slipping out of my hands. My players didn't know I existed.

How did everything become so complicated?

"Some spring break," I muttered.

I stayed at Abby's the rest of the afternoon. She tried so hard to make me feel better. She convinced Anna to play me some fiddle music she'd learned. That was cool. Then Abby called Claudia and invited her over. Claudia brought a new outfit she'd put together for the Blade concert. Abby and Anna both oohed and aahed over it. (To me, it looked like something Cinderella might have thrown out.)

Claudia offered to take me shopping for the concert. I said no way, José.

By the time I went home for dinner, my mood had lifted a little. As I walked up the front lawn, the Junk Bucket was pulling out of the driveway.

Mom was on the porch, waving to Charlie.

"Where's he going?" I asked.

"Out on a date," Mom replied with a smile. "Some new girlfriend."

"Cool," I said.

I walked inside. I went straight to the kitchen. Calmly, coolly, I helped prepare dinner.

I was determined not to be upset about anything. Okay, so now Charlie was dating Angelica. It was official. Sarah was a thing of the past. No big surprise.

It was my brother's life. Not my concern.

From now on, I was going to mind my own business.

Read all the books
about **Claudia**
in the Baby-sitters Club series
by Ann M. Martin

THE BABY-SITTERS CLUB®

Collect 'em all!

100 (and more)
Reasons to Stay Friends Forever!

☐ MG43388-1	#1	Kristy's Great Idea	$3.50
☐ MG43387-3	#10	Logan Likes Mary Anne!	$3.99
☐ MG43717-8	#15	Little Miss Stoneybrook...and Dawn	$3.50
☐ MG43722-4	#20	Kristy and the Walking Disaster	$3.50
☐ MG43347-4	#25	Mary Anne and the Search for Tigger	$3.50
☐ MG42498-X	#30	Mary Anne and the Great Romance	$3.50
☐ MG42508-0	#35	Stacey and the Mystery of Stoneybrook	$3.50
☐ MG44082-9	#40	Claudia and the Middle School Mystery	$3.25
☐ MG43574-4	#45	Kristy and the Baby Parade	$3.50
☐ MG44969-9	#50	Dawn's Big Date	$3.50
☐ MG44968-0	#51	Stacey's Ex-Best Friend	$3.50
☐ MG44966-4	#52	Mary Anne + 2 Many Babies	$3.50
☐ MG44967-2	#53	Kristy for President	$3.25
☐ MG44965-6	#54	Mallory and the Dream Horse	$3.25
☐ MG44964-8	#55	Jessi's Gold Medal	$3.25
☐ MG45657-1	#56	Keep Out, Claudia!	$3.50
☐ MG45658-X	#57	Dawn Saves the Planet	$3.50
☐ MG45659-8	#58	Stacey's Choice	$3.50
☐ MG45660-1	#59	Mallory Hates Boys (and Gym)	$3.50
☐ MG45662-8	#60	Mary Anne's Makeover	$3.50
☐ MG45663-6	#61	Jessi and the Awful Secret	$3.50
☐ MG45664-4	#62	Kristy and the Worst Kid Ever	$3.50
☐ MG45665-2	#63	Claudia's ~~Freind~~ Friend	$3.50
☐ MG45666-0	#64	Dawn's Family Feud	$3.50
☐ MG45667-9	#65	Stacey's Big Crush	$3.50
☐ MG47004-3	#66	Maid Mary Anne	$3.50
☐ MG47005-1	#67	Dawn's Big Move	$3.50
☐ MG47006-X	#68	Jessi and the Bad Baby-sitter	$3.50
☐ MG47007-8	#69	Get Well Soon, Mallory!	$3.50
☐ MG47008-6	#70	Stacey and the Cheerleaders	$3.50
☐ MG47009-4	#71	Claudia and the Perfect Boy	$3.99
☐ MG47010-8	#72	Dawn and the We ♥ Kids Club	$3.99
☐ MG47011-6	#73	Mary Anne and Miss Priss	$3.99
☐ MG47012-4	#74	Kristy and the Copycat	$3.99
☐ MG47013-2	#75	Jessi's Horrible Prank	$3.50
☐ MG47014-0	#76	Stacey's Lie	$3.50
☐ MG48221-1	#77	Dawn and Whitney, Friends Forever	$3.99
☐ MG48222-X	#78	Claudia and Crazy Peaches	$3.50
☐ MG48223-8	#79	Mary Anne Breaks the Rules	$3.50
☐ MG48224-6	#80	Mallory Pike, #1 Fan	$3.99
☐ MG48225-4	#81	Kristy and Mr. Mom	$3.50

More titles... ▶

❏ MG48226-2	#82	Jessi and the Troublemaker	$3.99
❏ MG48235-1	#83	Stacey vs. the BSC	$3.50
❏ MG48228-9	#84	Dawn and the School Spirit War	$3.50
❏ MG48236-X	#85	Claudi Kishi, Live from WSTO	$3.50
❏ MG48227-0	#86	Mary Anne and Camp BSC	$3.50
❏ MG48237-8	#87	Stacey and the Bad Girls	$3.50
❏ MG22872-2	#88	Farewell, Dawn	$3.50
❏ MG22873-0	#89	Kristy and the Dirty Diapers	$3.50
❏ MG22874-9	#90	Welcome to the BSC, Abby	$3.99
❏ MG22875-1	#91	Claudia and the First Thanksgiving	$3.50
❏ MG22876-5	#92	Mallory's Christmas Wish	$3.50
❏ MG22877-3	#93	Mary Anne and the Memory Garden	$3.99
❏ MG22878-1	#94	Stacey McGill, Super Sitter	$3.99
❏ MG22879-X	#95	Kristy + Bart = ?	$3.99
❏ MG22880-3	#96	Abby's Lucky Thirteen	$3.99
❏ MG22881-1	#97	Claudia and the World's Cutest Baby	$3.99
❏ MG22882-X	#98	Dawn and Too Many Sitters	$3.99
❏ MG69205-4	#99	Stacey's Broken Heart	$3.99
❏ MG69206-2	#100	Kristy's Worst Idea	$3.99
❏ MG69207-0	#101	Claudia Kishi, Middle School Dropout	$3.99
❏ MG69208-9	#102	Mary Anne and the Little Princess	$3.99
❏ MG69209-7	#103	Happy Holidays, Jessi	$3.99
❏ MG45575-3		Logan's Story Special Edition Readers' Request	$3.25
❏ MG47118-X		Logan Bruno, Boy Baby-sitter Special Edition Readers' Request	$3.50
❏ MG47756-0		Shannon's Story Special Edition	$3.50
❏ MG47686-6		The Baby-sitters Club Guide to Baby-sitting	$3.25
❏ MG47314-X		The Baby-sitters Club Trivia and Puzzle Fun Book	$2.50
❏ MG48400-1		BSC Portrait Collection: Claudia's Book	$3.50
❏ MG22864-1		BSC Portrait Collection: Dawn's Book	$3.50
❏ MG69181-3		BSC Portrait Collection: Kristy's Book	$3.99
❏ MG22865-X		BSC Portrait Collection: Mary Anne's Book	$3.99
❏ MG48399-4		BSC Portrait Collection: Stacey's Book	$3.50
❏ MG92713-2		The Complete Guide to The Baby-sitters Club	$4.95
❏ MG47151-1		The Baby-sitters Club Chain Letter	$14.95
❏ MG48295-5		The Baby-sitters Club Secret Santa	$14.95
❏ MG45074-3		The Baby-sitters Club Notebook	$2.50
❏ MG44783-1		The Baby-sitters Club Postcard Book	$4.95

Available wherever you buy books...or use this order form.
Scholastic Inc., P.O. Box 7502, 2931 E. McCarty Street, Jefferson City, MO 65102

Please send me the books I have checked above. I am enclosing $_____
(please add $2.00 to cover shipping and handling). Send check or money order–
no cash or C.O.D.s please.

Name_____ Birthdate_____

Address _____

City_____ State/Zip _____

BSC5962

The New THE BABY-SITTERS CLUB® FAN CLUB

Only $8.95! Plus $2.00 Postage and Handling

Sign up now for a year of great friendships and terrific memories!

★ **110-mm camera!**
Take photos of your pals!

★ **Mini-photo album**
Fill it with your best pics!

★ **Diary (with lock!)**
For your favorite memories...and secret thoughts!

★ **Stationery note cards and stickers**
Send letters to your far-away friends!

★ **Eight cool pencils**
With the signatures of different baby-sitters!

★ **Full-color BSC poster**

★ **Subscription to the official BSC newsletter***

★ **Special keepsake shipper**

Amazing stuff!

To get your fan club pack (in the U.S. and Canada only), just fill out the coupon or write the information on a 3" x 5" card and send it to us with your check or money order. U.S. residents: $8.95 plus $2.00 postage and handling to The New BSC FAN CLUB, Scholastic Inc. P.O. Box 7500, 2931 East McCarty Street, Jefferson City, MO 65102. Canadian residents: $13.95 plus $2.00 postage and handling to The New BSC FAN CLUB, Scholastic Canada, 123 Newkirk Road, Richmond Hill, Ontario, L4C3G5. Offer expires 9/30/97. Offer good for one year from date of receipt. Please allow 4-6 weeks for your introductory pack to arrive.

*First newsletter is sent after introductory pack. You will receive at least 4 newsletters during your one-year membership.

✂ - ✂

rry! Send me my New Baby-sitters Club Fan Club Pack. I am enclosing my check or ney order (no cash please) for U.S. residents: $10.95 ($8.95 plus $2.00) and for adian residents: $15.95 ($13.95 plus $2.00).

me_____ Birthdate_____
    First   Last   D/M/Y

dress_____

_____ State_____Zip_____

ephone ( )_____ Boy_____Girl_____

ere did you buy this book? ❑ Bookstore ❑ Book Fair ❑ Book Club ❑ Other_____

OLASTIC

B106397